Are You Thinking What I'm Thinking?

By Belle Payton

Simon Spotlight

New York London Toronto Sydney New Delhi

SIMON SPOTLIGHT
An imprint of Simon & Schuster Children's Publishing Division
1230 Avenue of the Americas, New York, New York 10020
This Simon Spotlight paperback edition July 2015
© 2015 by Simon & Schuster, Inc.
All rights reserved, including the right of reproduction in whole or in part in any form.
SIMON SPOTLIGHT and colophon are registered trademarks of Simon & Schuster, Inc.
For information about special discounts for bulk purchases, please contact Simon & Schuster Special Sales at 1-866-506-1949 or business@simonandschuster.com.
Text by Heather Alexander
Designed by Ciara Gay
The text of this book was set in Garamond.
Manufactured in the United States of America 0615 OFF
10 9 8 7 6 5 4 3 2 1
ISBN 978-1-4814-3138-5 (hc)
ISBN 978-1-4814-3137-8 (pbk)
ISBN 978-1-4814-3139-2 (eBook)
Library of Congress Catalog Card Number 2014945738

CHAPTER ONE

"I knew it," Alex Sackett declared. "I just knew it!"

"Knew what?" Ella Sanchez asked.

"That it was going to rain," Alex said. "It's pouring." She pointed toward the huge windows bordering Ashland Middle School's front door.

Ella peered through the rain-splattered glass. "Wow. It really is. Who knew?"

"I did!" Alex cried. "I sensed it this morning. I had this cute outfit planned, very nautical. Navy-and-white-striped top, navy pants, and my new red suede ballet flats. But I changed to a sweatshirt and sneakers. Ava said I was nuts, because the sun was shining when we left the house."

"So she didn't change her outfit too?" Ella asked, pulling her dark hair into a ponytail.

"Hello? Have you met my twin sister?" Alex asked with a laugh. "She was already wearing jeans and a sweatshirt. Ava wears the same outfit practically every day, rain or shine."

Ella shook her head. "I don't have any classes with Ava. Why doesn't she do debate club with us?"

"It's not really her thing," Alex replied. She and Ella had just left the after-school meeting of the debate club. Although they'd gotten to know each other a little when they were both running for seventh-grade class president, they weren't close friends. But after watching Ella outdebate an eighth grader on why America needs a female president, Alex knew that would change. Especially because Ella had been really nice to Alex when Alex won the election.

Alex loved debate club. She loved sharing ideas and talking in front of a group. But Ava didn't—she loved sports. And she was good at them too. She was the only girl on the Ashland Tiger Cubs football team.

"Any sign of the late bus?" Ella asked.

Alex pressed her nose to the glass. The wind

caused the trees to sway and the rain to pelt sideways. "Nothing yellow out there," she reported. "No bus yet."

Boom!

Alex jumped at the loud clap. Her eyes widened as a jagged streak of lightning slashed through the sky.

Ella squealed. "So cool! I love thunderstorms. I wonder if it will turn into a tornado."

Alex bit her lip and tried to slow her thudding heart. She didn't think the storm was cool. Far from it.

Her family was still new to Texas. They had moved here over the summer from Massachusetts so her dad could coach the high school football team. Before a scary tornado hit a few weeks back, Alex had never been in a tornado. It had been horrible. She and Ava had to take cover in their bathtub!

She really hoped she wouldn't be in a second one.

Alex's eyes darted between the storm outside and the clock over the main office door. The bus was supposed to be there soon.

More kids gathered to wait, and snippets of their conversations swirled around her.

"Mr. Antonucci is giving a social studies test tomorrow."

"Have you seen that new app?"

". . . and then my mother said . . ."

Even with all the kids and noise, a lonely feeling suddenly overcame her. She wished Ava were by her side, like she had been during the last storm.

But Ava was at football practice in the gym. Sports let out after clubs, and the special sports bus left after the late bus. Ava would be on that bus.

Should I wait for Ava? Alex wondered.

She debated finding an excuse to stay at school longer so she could ride the bus with her sister. Maybe she could talk to Ms. Palmer about student council plans. But then she remembered she had seen Ms. Palmer leave before she went into debate club.

Stop it, she scolded herself. No one else seemed to be scared by this storm. It probably wasn't a big deal. She should just get on the late bus without Ava.

Think logically. She liked logic and facts and figures. *Not every storm is a tornado,* she reminded herself.

Alex flattened her palm against the window and peered out. The sky had grown dark.

4

Another crash of thunder boomed. The lightning flashed so close, it illuminated her hand. Alex stifled a shriek.

This isn't about logic, she thought. This was about fear.

She really wished Ava were here to ride the bus home with her.

At that moment, in the window's reflection, Alex saw double. Green eyes like hers, pale skin with light freckles like hers, and curly, chocolate-brown hair like hers. Except this girl's hair was cropped to her chin, while Alex's fell past her shoulders.

"Ava!" Alex cried, and whirled around. She'd wished for her twin sister, and now she was here. A shiver ran down Alex's spine.

"Are you okay?" Ava asked. She hoisted her backpack onto her left shoulder and tilted her head at her twin.

"I'm fine . . . I'm totally fine," Alex said. She let out the breath she hadn't realized she'd been holding. "What are you doing here?"

"Coach Kenerson called practice early," Ava explained. "Because of the rain. I'm taking the late bus with you."

"That's so strange—" Alex began.

"The bus is here!" Ella called.

"Come on! Let's run for it," Ava said. She headed out the door with the crowd of kids, and Alex followed.

As they sprinted through the sheets of rain, Alex grabbed her sister's hand. Together they boarded the bus, dripping puddles down the aisle as they made their way toward the back.

They slid into the seat behind Corey O'Sullivan and Jack Valdeavano. Raindrops fell from Corey's red hair. With a mischievous look, he gave his head an aggressive shake, spraying the twins.

"Gross! What are you, a wet dog?" Ava cried.

"Top dog," he boasted. "I'm your quarterback, remember? The star of the Tiger Cubs?"

"Conceited much?" Alex teased. Corey wasn't actually conceited, but he did have a great throwing arm and, as far as Alex was concerned, an even better smile.

"Just telling it like it is," Corey joked, puffing out his chest.

"It's so sad. The rain got into his brain," Jack said.

"From all the holes in his head," Ava added with a grin.

"Score!" Jack held up his hand. Ava slapped his palm. Corey and Alex collapsed into giggles.

Ava continued to joke with Corey and Jack as the bus pulled out of the school parking lot. Ava played football with Corey and hung out with Jack a lot, shooting hoops at the nearby park. She had an easy way with boys that Alex envied—without Ava around, Alex wouldn't have known what to say to Jack and Corey.

The bus's headlights cut through the storm as it turned down another street.

Thunder boomed in the distance. The rain drumming against the bus's roof made Alex's skin tingle.

"It's spooky out there," she said.

"Spooky is good," Jack said. "We need to make next weekend spooky. But with no rain."

"What's next weekend?" Ava asked.

"Halloween," Alex answered.

"Not just Halloween," Corey said. "Lindsey's party."

"It's going to be epic," Jack agreed.

Alex nodded, but her brain was spinning. Lindsey Davis was having a party? How could she not know this? Weren't she and Lindsey close friends?

"Is it a costume party?" Ava asked.

"Is there any other kind for Halloween?" Corey asked. "I helped Lindz come up with all these wacky categories. Makes My Little Sister Cry. Weirdest Superhero. Most Likely to Get the Most Likes. The winning costumes get prizes."

Alex chewed her lip. *It's not strange that Corey knows all this about the party,* she told herself. *Lindsey and Corey are going out. Still . . . could I really not be invited?*

"Lindsey told us about it at lunch," Jack said.

Aha! Alex had missed lunch today to make signs for the student council car wash. "So are we all invited?"

She had to ask, just to be extra sure.

"I think you're the one with water in the brain," Corey said to Alex. "Of course we're all invited. Practically the whole seventh grade is invited!"

Alex nodded, as if she already knew this.

"I heard Sloane promised to make food for the party," Jack offered. Lindsey's older sister Sloane had graduated high school and was now in culinary school.

"And I'm going to eat it all!" Corey cried. "Sloane makes these insane pumpkin cupcakes with cream filling. Lindsey should do a cupcake-eating contest. I'd win."

"I want to win one of the costume prizes," Ava said.

"Me too," Alex agreed. "I always plan my Halloween costume in July. I have a really original one this year."

"Not me," Ava said. "I always wait until the last minute. But I came up with an idea this morning."

"So what are you guys going to be?" Jack asked.

"A Spelling Bee!" Alex and Ava said at the same time.

Alex met Ava's surprised gaze. Another shiver ran down her spine.

"Together?" Jack asked.

"No, not together." Alex pulled her fingers through her damp hair. She didn't recall ever telling Ava her idea. How could they have come up with the exact same costume?

"What is a Spelling Bee?" Corey asked.

"I'm going to wearing a cute bumblebee outfit. Yellow and black with wings and a stinger," Alex explained. "Then I'm going to attach letters from the alphabet to my bee body. Get it? Spelling Bee?"

Corey groaned. "Leave it to the Sackett twins to make Halloween complicated. Ever hear of a witch or a ghost?"

"Boring," Ava said. "Alex and I definitely don't do boring."

"And you're going to make the same bee costume as Alex?" Jack asked Ava.

Ava shrugged. "The idea just randomly popped into my mind. But yeah, sure. It would be funny if we were twin bees." Ava laughed, and Corey and Jack joined in.

"*Spelling* bees," Alex corrected her.

But already her mind was spinning. She and Ava had always chosen costumes that were totally different. Once she'd been a princess and Ava had been a dragon slayer. The year she was a bunny, Ava was a dinosaur. Last year Alex had gone as an angel and Ava had decided on Halloween morning to go as a devil. So why this year had they all of a sudden picked the same costume?

Her dad would say they'd had one of their "twin connections" today. That's what he called it when they had the same ideas or said the same thing. But this was their first Halloween with their new friends in Ashland. Alex loved

Ava, but there was no way they were appearing at Lindsey's party dressed in the same costume!

Ava stepped off the bus and gazed at the sky. The rain had slowed, and the storm seemed to be passing.

"I wish I had an umbrella," Alex grumbled as she stepped off behind Ava.

"Our house is only down the block." Ava shrugged. She didn't care about wet hair the way her twin did.

"Only?" Alex sighed and walked alongside Ava. Suddenly she stopped. "Why did you steal my costume idea?"

"What?" Ava asked.

"You know what," Alex said, still not moving. "Somehow you found out about my Spelling Bee idea, and then you stole it."

"I didn't steal it. I promise," Ava said. "Come on, let's get home."

"No, wait! Prove it. How did you come up with Spelling Bee at that exact moment?" Alex asked.

Ava pointed to the yellow-and-black Pittsburgh Steelers jersey she wore. "At breakfast, Mom said

I looked like a bumblebee. And I was in the middle of going over words for my spelling test. So I thought of a Spelling Bee. Mystery solved."

Alex eyed her suspiciously. "Fine, but it was my idea first. You can't be it too."

"Why not?" Ava asked, heading down the sidewalk. She had no intention of being a Spelling Bee now, but she liked teasing Alex.

"Because you don't even like spelling!" Alex sputtered.

"You don't even like bees," Ava countered.

Alex's face grew red, and she stalked toward home.

Ava followed, letting out an occasional *"bzzz, bzzz"* to annoy her sister.

"Mom!" Alex called, pulling open their front door. "Mom! Make her stop!"

"Bzzzz!" Ava teased as she trailed Alex into the kitchen. Their mom was washing the breakfast dishes. Ava suspected she had been in her ceramics studio in their garage since they'd left this morning. Mrs. Sackett's ceramics business had recently taken off. She had already sold one hundred little blue-glazed pots.

"Mom, tell Ava she can't be a Spelling Bee," Alex demanded.

"You want to be in a spelling bee, Ave?" Mrs. Sacket raised her eyebrows in surprise. "That is so exciting! Did your teacher ask you?"

"Not that kind of spelling bee," Ava said. She hated to disappoint her mom, but spelling was definitely not her thing. She had barely managed to pull out a C on her last spelling quiz. But now wasn't the time to share that news.

Alex quickly explained as their dad and their older brother, Tommy, pushed open the back door. Moxy, their Australian shepherd, ran to greet them. She got the most excited when Coach came home.

"We ended practice early because of the rain," Coach said.

"Well, I'm glad you're home. We can all have dinner together," said Mrs. Sackett. Family dinners were rare during football season—especially on a Friday night.

"I'm not glad. The play-off game is a week from tomorrow," Coach grumbled. "We need the practice."

"That's not the only thing next week," Ava reminded him. "It's your birthday on Sunday!"

"It'll be a busy weekend," Mrs. Sackett said. "And the big game is on Halloween! It's fun that they're doing the game on a Saturday afternoon instead of Friday night. The fans are supposed to come in costume. And then Dad's birthday the day after."

"What do you want for your birthday?" Alex asked him. She loved shopping for gifts. *Shopping for anything, really,* Ava thought.

"How about a party?" Tommy suggested.

"No way!" Coach said. "No gifts. No party. All I want is for the team to win the play-off game."

He clipped a leash onto Moxy's collar. "I know you hate the rain, girl, but you need a little exercise. Let's go run a few plays."

"Poor Moxy," Tommy said, as Coach left with their dog.

"Listen," Ava said. "We need to plan something for his birthday. We have to celebrate."

"But if the Tigers lose . . ." Alex didn't finish her thought.

No one said anything. They all knew it would be a horribly depressing birthday if the team lost the game.

CHAPTER TWO

"Alex, you're the best," Emily Campbell gushed. "Lindsey wouldn't come with me."

"It's no big deal," Alex said. "I love the mall. Besides, Lindsey is probably busy getting ready for her party."

Lindsey had texted Alex and Ava last night with official invites. Alex's eyes darted around the Ashland Mall, searching for inspiration for a new costume. Even though Ava had assured her she wouldn't also be a Spelling Bee, Alex had decided to come up with something else. She wasn't sure if she was going for scary or pretty. Either way, she wanted to look spectacular at the party.

"Lindsey thinks I'm obsessed with Madame Sibyl, just because I binge watch both her TV shows, but I'm not." Emily defiantly pushed her straight blond hair behind her ears.

"Wow!" Alex took a closer look at her friend. "Both of them?"

"Totally. I've seen every episode of each at least three times. Madame Sibyl is amazing. She can see into the future and talk to the dead. Don't you love her too?" Emily asked.

"She's fun to watch," Alex agreed. She and Ava had watched Madame Sibyl's reality show, but they always ended up laughing at the psychic. All her predictions seemed pretty wild.

"I can't believe she's here signing her new book at the Book Nook. I so want to meet her and get her autograph!" Emily bounced with excitement. "Don't you? And you can get one for Ava."

"Sure," Alex said uncertainly. She didn't tell Emily, but Ava had refused to come along. She said she didn't want an autograph of a charlatan. Alex had taught Ava that word last week. Alex loved vocabulary words. She collected them the way some girls collected nail polish or lip gloss. And she always shared her new words with her family—whether they wanted to hear them or not.

Alex wasn't sure whether Madame Sibyl was a charlatan, or a fake, but she was happy to keep Emily company. And go shopping.

"The signing doesn't start for another fifteen minutes. Can we make a detour?" Alex asked.

"I don't want to be late," Emily replied.

"Pretty please? I'll be fast. I need to get my dad a birthday present." Alex pointed to Mangia Bene, a store with brightly colored kitchen utensils. Baking was her dad's second love, after football.

"Okay, but let's hurry," said Emily, ushering Alex into the store.

Alex walked quickly through the aisles, inspecting baking pans, waffle makers, and food processors. "This store is making me hungry," she said. "We should go eat."

"No way! Madame Sibyl is only here for a short time," Emily reminded her.

"One more second," Alex said, still searching. Then she whooped when she spotted the perfect gift. She held up a football-shaped spatula. "Dad will flip! Get it?"

"Got it. It's excellent," Emily agreed. "Now buy it. Come on!"

Alex quickly paid, and they raced to the bookstore. A line snaked around the signing area. They stood behind an old woman with white hair and hot-pink sneakers.

Alex craned her neck to see Madame Sibyl. She was young and fashionable. Her ebony hair was piled in a messy topknot, and she wore scarlet lipstick, but she looked smaller in person than on TV.

"This is going to take a while," Alex said. "I'm hungry. How about I run to the food court and get us some snacks?"

"Oh, no! You have to wait with me. You can't miss meeting her," Emily said. "Besides, the line's moving fast."

Alex groaned. "I may wither without food," she half joked.

"Hello, girls," a bookstore employee greeted them. He was dressed in all black except for green cowboy boots. His name tag read HANK. "I'm selling Madame Sibyl's book, so you're all ready to go when it's your turn to get her autograph."

"Oh, yes!" Emily cried, pulling money from her wallet.

"How about you?" Hank held a thick book out to Alex.

"No, thanks," she said.

"Why not, Alex?" Emily asked.

"She's not my thing. I'll read yours," Alex promised.

"No one's touching my book after Madame Sibyl touches it!" Emily warned.

Suddenly Alex understood why Lindsey said Emily was obsessed.

"I'll just say hi to her then." Alex waved Hank away.

"I wonder what she'll tell me." Emily stared at the book's glossy cover. *The Power* was written in bold silver letters. "I hope she sees good things in my future."

"A boyfriend? Fame? Fortune?" Alex asked.

"All of it and more!" Emily giggled.

"Watch out, world, here comes Emily!" Alex teased. "Soon you'll be on the cover of every magazine from Hollywood to New York."

"Wait, I almost forgot. I have news," Emily said. "There's going to be a new girl in school on Monday. And she's from New York City!"

"How do you know that?" Alex asked.

"Mrs. Schiller told Mrs. Navarro, and Mrs. Navarro told my mom," Emily explained.

"Of course!" Alex laughed. Moms were always

warning their kids not to gossip, yet they seemed to gossip most of all. "So who is she?"

"Her name is Charlotte Huang. That's all I really know. I bet she'll be cool, since she's from New York," Emily said.

"Really? And what did you think I was going to be like when you heard I was moving here from Massachusetts?" Alex asked playfully.

"Oh, super cool," Emily assured her. "Actually, we thought it was cool that your dad was coming back to Texas to coach football."

Alex nodded. Her dad had grown up in Texas.

"Ohhh!" Emily suddenly squealed. "We're next."

Alex stood next to Emily as they approached the table. Madame Sibyl wore tight white jeans, a sparkly silver tank top, and strappy silver heels. Alex thought she looked totally cute—but a little overdressed for a Saturday afternoon book signing in a mall.

"Girls, girls, how wonderful of you to come. I love my young fans," Madame Sibyl said, reaching for Emily's book.

Her throaty voice sounded the same as it did on TV. Alex had never been this close to a TV star before.

"C-can you sign it to Emily? That's me," Emily said quietly. "I, uh, watch your show."

Alex gazed at her friend in surprise. Was Emily nervous?

"She has watched *all* your shows a *zillion* times!" Alex blurted out.

"A true fan!" Sibyl smiled. "I will write that."

Emily blushed and stared wide-eyed as Sibyl's pen scrawled across the book's title page.

"And what about you?" Sibyl turned her gaze to Alex. "Not a true fan?"

"Uh, no, I mean, I watch . . ." Alex fumbled.

"But you didn't buy a book?"

Now it was Alex's turn to blush. "Moral support. I came along for my friend."

Madame Sibyl arched one thin eyebrow. "I would think a girl like you would be interested in my book."

"Excuse me?" Alex said.

"You are a good friend. But you are an even better sister, no?" Madame Sibyl's voice was so low, Alex had to lean forward.

"What?" A nervous giggle escaped Alex's lips.

"You are strong, my dear, but together with your twin you are even stronger." Sibyl's dark eyes bored into Alex's.

A familiar shiver made its way down Alex's back. "How do you know I'm a twin?" she asked.

"I can sense we share the Power, but yours is twice as strong because there are two of you. The Power of Two." She reached out and grabbed both of Alex's hands. "Can't you feel it?"

Alex pulled back and blinked rapidly. Beside her, Emily gasped.

"Sibyl?" Hank stepped in between them. "You're scheduled for a break. There's coffee in the manager's office." He turned to the rest of the line. "She'll be back soon, y'all."

Alex stared after Sibyl as she followed Hank to the back of the store.

Suddenly the air grew hot and suffocating. Alex's lungs contracted and her hands shook. She needed to get out. Whirling around, she headed for the exit that led into the mall.

"Oh my God. Oh my God," Emily repeated as she followed Alex.

"What was that all about?" Alex asked, stopping next to the indoor fountain. She took several deep, calming breaths. Nearby, a little boy tossed a penny in for luck.

"She connected with you," Emily said in awe.

"I have no idea what that means," Alex scoffed.

"She psychically sensed that you were a twin," Emily said.

Alex shook her head. "Oh, please! We're in Ashland. Everyone in this town knows I'm one of Coach Sackett's twin daughters."

Emily pointed to the bio written on the book's back cover. "Sibyl isn't from Texas. She's from Louisiana."

Alex gulped. She didn't have an answer for that.

"She said you have powers." Emily began bouncing on her toes with excitement. "Do you? Have you ever done anything psychic?"

"Of course not!" Alex laughed. "The woman is a fraud."

But as she said it, she thought back to yesterday. Wishing for Ava in the storm. The Spelling Bee.

Her stomach tightened.

"That would be so cool if you had the Power like Madame Sibyl," Emily said.

"I don't," Alex said. "I wish Ava were here. She would have totally laughed at Sibyl."

At that moment, her phone dinged. Alex gazed at the incoming text.

"It's from Ava," she said quietly.

"What?" cried Emily. "What does it say?"

Alex could barely get the words out. "Ava's text says, 'I'm here.'"

Emily sucked in her breath. "Whoa! You just wished that! You and Ava do have the Power!"

Alex texted back.

Where are you???

Mom and I are waiting in the car by the door next to the art supply store. Hurry up. I'm hungry!!!!

Alex let out a loud laugh. She showed Emily the text. "The only power Ava and I share is the need to eat!"

CHAPTER THREE

Ava stared at the yellow slip of paper instructing her to go to the principal's office.

It was Monday morning. She had just walked into homeroom. What could she have possibly done? Her mind raced through the possibilities. She had turned in all her homework last week. She hadn't been late to practice at all. She always threw away her trash at lunch.

"Ava?" Ms. Kerry tapped her shoulder. "Are you okay?"

Ava forced a smile. "I hope so. I guess I should go, huh?"

Her teacher nodded, and Ava headed to Ms. Farmen's office. She had been there only twice:

on her first day of school, and when she was fighting the school board to let her play football.

Mrs. Gusman, the school secretary, was on the phone. She smiled broadly at Ava and pointed toward Ms. Farmen's door.

If I were getting in trouble, Mrs. Gusman wouldn't smile. Right? Ava reasoned.

Unless the secretary was evil.

But Ava didn't think she was. Mrs. Gusman was known for handing out hard butterscotch candies to the kids.

Ava cautiously pushed open the principal's door. An amazing-looking girl stood next to Ms. Farmen. She had caramel-colored skin, almond-shaped eyes, and brown hair that cascaded down her back. She wore skinny jeans, a sheer white shirt that revealed a red tank, and lots of silver jewelry.

"This is Ava Sackett," Ms. Farmen said. "Ava, this is Charlotte Huang. Charlotte is new to our school."

"Hey," Ava said, still confused.

Charlotte gave a forced smile.

"Ava, I've chosen you to be Charlotte's buddy today. I'd like you to help her find her classes and her locker. Introduce her around," Ms. Farmen explained.

"Me?" Ava asked. She wondered if the principal had sent for the wrong twin by mistake. Alex was on the student council. She was the one teachers picked to do this kind of thing. "But I'm still new here too."

"Exactly!" Ms. Farmen cried. "I thought you'd be perfect for this honor. You remember what it feels like, and all your teachers say you've been fitting in well and are easy to get along with. Here are passes to be late to first period. Give Charlotte the grand tour!"

Before Ava could respond, she and Charlotte were guided into the hall, and Ms. Farmen turned her attention to Kal Tippett, who was waiting by her door. From his angry pose and his defiant expression, Ava suspected Kal was in trouble.

And she'd been given an honor. Pretty cool!

"Why don't I walk you around the school?" Ava suggested to Charlotte.

"Sure. Fine," Charlotte said, not looking at Ava. She shuffled down the hallway, barely acknowledging the classrooms and teachers Ava pointed out.

Hmmm, I better channel my inner Alex, Ava thought. "So, where did you move from?" she asked Charlotte brightly.

"New York City," Charlotte said defiantly. "This is my first time moving."

"It was mine, too. Alex and I had always gone to the same school before we moved here this summer. We used to live just outside Boston," Ava said, scanning Charlotte's schedule. "Moving is a huge deal."

"You're from Boston? And who's Alex?" Charlotte asked, looking up at Ava for the first time.

"She's my twin. We're identical, but that's biological. We like different stuff and do different things." Ava glanced at Charlotte's outfit. "I think you'll really like Alex."

"I think I'll like both of you," Charlotte said, peering into the empty cafeteria. "We could be the three East Coast girls."

"We could," Ava agreed. *There we go!* she thought. *I'm getting her to open up.* "But I bet our little Boston suburb was a lot different from living in New York City."

"This is all very different," Charlotte muttered, looking away again.

"The school?"

"The whole Texas thing. It's hard to take it all in," Charlotte said.

"I hear you. When I first moved, it felt like we'd

landed on a different planet. Texas is very . . . well"—Ava wasn't sure how to describe it—"very Texas. But you get used to it."

"I hope not!" Charlotte said. Then, apologetically, "My parents sprang the moving thing on me." She was quiet for a moment. "So tell me about Ashland."

"Well, what do you think about football?" Ava asked.

Charlotte shrugged. "I'm not really into sports, unless you count ballet. I like to dance."

"That's not going to fly here in Texas," Ava said, laughing.

"For real?" Charlotte looked panicked. "I know nothing about football."

"You'll have to learn," Ava said. "The Friday night high school games are a huge deal. It's touchdowns instead of tutus for you now." She grinned.

Charlotte frowned. "Friday night in my family is movie night. We see new movies on opening weekend. An air-conditioned movie theater sounds way sweeter than a hot stadium."

"You're right about the heat. Texas is crazy hot!" Ava said.

"It's like living with a hair dryer constantly

blasting on you," Charlotte agreed, laughing. Then she got quiet again. "I'm going to miss snow. And the city. Walking to the French bakery on the corner. My doorman. My apartment."

They wandered down several halls in uncomfortable silence.

"And what's with all the barbecue places?" Charlotte asked suddenly. "Every restaurant in town is barbecue or burritos. I bet they put barbecue sauce in their sushi down here!"

"Now you're getting the picture!" Ava laughed. It had taken her a while to get used to all these things too. Charlotte would be fine. "And don't forget the cowboy boots and hats."

"The only way I could see myself rocking a pair of cowboy boots is if they're red," Charlotte said. "And only in a sarcastic kind of way."

Ava wasn't sure what she meant. She'd never worn her clothes in any special kind of way.

"Oh, hey, do you have boots?" Charlotte asked. "I'm really sorry, I didn't mean to put you down."

"You didn't. I haven't bought boots yet," Ava confessed. Although she had thought about it last week for the first time, now that it was getting a little cooler.

"I told you! We're East Coast girls. We need to stick together," Charlotte said. "I'm glad I met you."

"Me too," Ava said. Charlotte seemed really sweet, and Ava knew what it was like to be homesick. "Listen, I could teach you about football," she offered. She explained that she played on the boys' team.

"I'm going to pass," Charlotte said. "I'm not going to need that knowledge. Ever."

Ava wasn't so sure about this—after all, most of the Ashland social scene revolved around football games, and Charlotte seemed like someone who'd want to be social. But she didn't want to harass the new girl on her first day.

"We could go see movies together, though," Charlotte said shyly.

"Sure!" said Ava. "And hey, do you want to sit with me at lunch?"

Charlotte's eyes brightened. "Thank you. Girls without boots need to stick together."

"That doesn't quite work," Ava admitted. "My friend Kylie, you'll meet her at lunch, always wears boots—she lives on a ranch."

"A ranch? Like with cows?" Charlotte asked.

"Not cows. In Texas they're called cattle.

Cows are the girls. Bulls are the boys," Ava said, strangely impressed that she now knew that.

Charlotte sighed. "I don't belong here."

"Don't say that. You'll make tons of friends," Ava promised. "Everyone will love you."

"Madame Sibyl said that Alex has the Power!" Emily announced to the entire lunch table on Monday.

"What's the Power?" Rosa Navarro asked before biting into her ham sandwich.

"Come on, Rosa. Haven't you watched the TV show?" Lindsey asked. "The Power is a psychic thing. You know, knowing things before they happen. Reading people's minds."

"You can do that?" Rosa asked Alex.

"She and Ava can do it together. That's what Madame Sibyl said," Emily proclaimed proudly. She wrapped her arm around Alex's shoulder and gave it a squeeze.

"Like how you guys said the same thing on the bus on Friday?" Corey asked.

All eyes turned to Alex. She was suddenly the center of attention. Lindsey had been the center of attention earlier when she'd described her Halloween party plans. Now everyone wanted to know about Alex's psychic abilities.

"Ava and I often have the same thoughts and say the same things. It's like we can read each other's minds," Alex explained. She avoided saying anything about the Power. She didn't believe what Madame Sibyl had said.

At least, she didn't think she did.

"But isn't mind reading a twin thing?" Annelise Mueller asked. Annelise was a cheerleader, along with Rosa, Lindsey, and Emily. Alex wasn't—she'd had a disastrous tryout—but she worked with them on their fund-raising and publicity. "Lots of twins do that."

"Well, sure—" Alex began.

"With Alex and Ava, it's something much more intense," Emily explained. "Tell us, Alex."

Everyone leaned forward, looking at her. Smiling at her. This was her chance to be someone more than the new girl or the do-gooder class president or Coach Sackett's daughter. To be someone exotic. Someone with the Power.

Alex tried to explain her and Ava's connection. It wasn't easy. She'd never put it into words before. It was just a feeling she'd always had.

She thought Ava felt it too, but she'd never asked her.

"So how does the Power work?" Logan Medina asked. "What do you do first?"

"It's not like a recipe you can follow," Emily scoffed.

"I don't know if it's really a power," Alex said hesitantly. "It just happens. We think the same things. And if we think something hard enough, it happens. Last week, I was thinking that I really wanted to see Ava, and then she showed up, even though I thought she was at football."

"Can you do it now?" Annelise asked.

"Yes!" Emily cried. "Do it now, Alex. Show us the Power!"

"Here?" Alex bit her lip.

"Totally!" Emily said. She pointed to a table across the cafeteria, where Ava sat with Kylie McClaire and a pretty girl whom Alex didn't recognize. "Use your mind to get Ava to come over here."

"Go for it!" cried Xander Browning. He pounded the tabletop.

Soon all the boys were pounding and chanting. "Show us the Power!"

"Okay, okay," Alex said shakily. She gazed at

Ava, hoping to give her some kind of signal. But Ava's back was toward Alex, and she seemed to be laughing at something Kylie had said.

How was she supposed to silently communicate with her twin on command? What had she gotten herself into?

"Are you doing it?" Emily whispered.

Alex nodded and closed her eyes.

"Shhh, guys," Emily whispered to the others.

Ava. Ava. Ava. Alex silently repeated her sister's name.

Could she somehow sneakily text Ava to hightail it over here? That seemed like the only way this would work. She opened one eye.

Everyone was watching her.

She closed her eye. What choice did she have? There was no logical way that Ava could receive her psychic message. Alex knew that. Whenever they'd had twin connections before, they'd always been together. And the past few days had just been full of coincidences.

This was going to end badly.

They'll all laugh at me, she realized. *By next period, I'll be the joke of the school.*

She came up with a plan. She'd keep her eyes closed until the bell rang. Maybe convince them that there hadn't been enough time. Or the conditions weren't ideal.

Or something.

She inhaled the pungent odor of tacos. She listened to distant laughter. And waited. And thought really, really hard about Ava.

Ava looked around the crowded cafeteria. The entire seventh grade was packed in. A strange odor of tacos and industrial cleaner filled the air.

"Here." Ava passed half her peanut butter and jelly sandwich and one of her dad's homemade oatmeal cookies to Kylie.

Kylie slid over her corn chips and a bunch of grapes.

Every day they shared the best parts of their lunch. It was much better than buying the cafeteria food.

"Do you want some?" Ava held up the bag of chips to Charlotte.

"Thanks." Charlotte nibbled on a chip. "Do you like Mallomars? I brought twenty boxes when we moved. I could bring some for us tomorrow."

"What are those?" Kylie asked.

"Chocolate-covered marshmallow cookies," Ava explained. "They're yummy. My mom likes them."

"It's an East Coast thing. You can only get them in our part of the country," Charlotte explained. "Right, Ava?"

"I didn't know that," Ava said. Had she seen the cookies here in Texas? She guessed not. She hadn't really missed them, though.

"So let me finish telling you who's who." Ava gazed at the nearby tables. They had been giving Charlotte the breakdown of all the groups at Ashland Middle School. "Okay, we've covered the drama kids, the band geeks, the A-plus kids, and the random table."

"So that leaves the sporty kids," Kylie said. "They're kind of divided. That table is the baseball and volleyball boys. That table is a mishmash—soccer girls, softball girls, and I think gymnasts and swimmers."

"And then there's football," Ava said.

"And cheerleaders," Kylie added with a knowing smile. "There's two tables of those mixed together, but one group is much cooler." She nodded her head in the direction of Alex's table. It was easy to see that they were the social center of the seventh grade. The energy of the room seemed to naturally swirl in their direction.

"Is that Alex?" Charlotte asked, surveying the table. "She looks like you, Ava."

"Indeed she does," Kylie answered. "See the cute boy at the end? The one with the dark hair and green shirt? We're sort of going out."

"Sort of?" Charlotte asked.

"His name is Owen," Ava explained. "They like each other, but each of them is too shy to do anything but text emojis."

"That's not true!" Kylie twirled one of her many tiny braids. "Okay, it is a little."

"So why don't you guys sit over there too?" Charlotte asked.

"Sometimes we do," Ava said. "But sometimes we just like to chill, the two of us. Three now." She smiled at Charlotte.

"That works for me," Charlotte said.

"And their table is really crowded." Kylie played with all the rings on her fingers as she thought about it some more. "And sometimes Owen gets weird when I sit near him. He can't seem to spit out a full sentence."

"Boys are like that," Charlotte said knowingly. Ava wondered if she'd had a boyfriend in her old school.

Charlotte watched the kids at Alex's table. "Alex looks nice. And pretty, too."

"Do you want to meet her?" Ava asked. "I *am* supposed to be introducing you around. I'll introduce you to the whole group."

Charlotte hesitated. "I can meet her later. With you."

"Let's go now," Kylie said, her dark eyes flashing mischievously.

"Oh, you want an excuse to say hi to Owen," Ava teased.

"I don't need an excuse," Kylie said. "I want to help you be a good ambassador."

"Likely story." Ava turned to Charlotte. "Come on."

Ava and Kylie led Charlotte across the cafeteria. As Ava drew closer, she saw that Alex had her eyes closed. What was she doing? Sleeping? Here?

"She's coming!" Emily let out a high-pitched squeal.

Alex's eyelids shot open. Her eyes bulged with surprise, and she leaped to her feet. "You're *here*!" she cried. "Ava, you're here!"

"Obviously," Ava said, tilting her head.

"That's amazing!" A huge smile lit up Alex's face. "I did it!"

"I told you!" Emily said.

"Way incredible!" Lindsey cried.

"I can't believe you just walked over," Corey said to Ava.

"Believe it," Ava said. "What's with all of you?"

"Alex just made you appear," Emily said. "It's the Power."

"I'm still not following." Ava turned to Alex, who had dropped back into her seat. Alex shrugged and chewed at her lip. Ava knew she was trying to work something out in her mind. Alex chewed her lip when she did math and when she had a problem. "So?" she asked.

Alex didn't say anything. Ava decided to wait until they were home to ask her about it.

"Okay, moving on," Ava said. "This is Charlotte. She's new and really nice. She's from New York City."

Everyone said hi, but Charlotte just stared down at her feet.

"Hey, I thought New Yorkers talked a lot," Corey teased.

Charlotte turned to him with a glare. Her many silver bracelets chimed together as she crossed her arms. Ava wasn't sure why she'd suddenly clammed up. Corey's comment was kind of rude, but he was just kidding. Maybe Charlotte couldn't see that.

Emily looked at Ava quizzically, and Ava shrugged. "Well, welcome to Texas, Charlotte," Emily said with a big smile and a nod at Ava.

"No 'Howdy, y'all'?" Charlotte asked finally. "I mean, isn't this cowboy country?" When she spoke, it was with a strange Southern twang that she hadn't used with Ava.

"This isn't cowboy country," Lindsey said defensively. "We have a mall, we're near a big city. Ashland isn't the middle of nowhere."

"Compared to New York it is," Charlotte mumbled. Ava looked at her in shock. It was one thing to complain about her new town to Ava, but to complain in front of all these kids who'd grown up here seemed mean.

"Hey, don't dis Texas," Corey protested. "Texas has football."

"And ranches," Kylie added.

"And Dr Pepper," Annelise put in.

"And you guys think those are good things?" Charlotte gave a sharp laugh that startled Ava even more. "Manhattan has museums, chic shopping, Broadway shows, and amazing restaurants. Texas is like Hicksville."

Doesn't she know that these kids love Texas? Ava wondered. She glanced at Alex, who didn't seem to be listening to Charlotte. She was gazing off toward some unseen spot, murmuring, "I did it. I really did it."

"I like your shirt, Charlotte," Emily tried again. "And your bracelets. Did you get them at the mall?"

"As if! These came from a little vintage store in the West Village. You don't have stores that cool anywhere in Texas," Charlotte said. Ava cringed.

"But we can order anything online," Lindsey pointed out. "I could order a shirt from Paris if I wanted to."

"But by the time the delivery guy makes it all the way out here, that shirt will be so last year!" Charlotte let out another short laugh.

Emily and Lindsey gave each other looks.

Ava groaned. Didn't Charlotte know that she was supposed to tell Emily how fabulous her shirt or shoes or something was? Emily and Lindsey were used to everyone complimenting them. If Charlotte had wanted to get in with the popular crowd, she'd messed up her first impression, Ava realized.

No, she'd more than messed it up.

She'd destroyed it.

CHAPTER FOUR

Ava stood in the middle of her bedroom and listened. She'd never heard her house this quiet on a weekday morning. Usually by the time her mom yelled that she'd be late, Ava could hear Coach making breakfast, Tommy singing in the shower, and Alex fiddling with her straightening iron as she recited vocabulary words.

But not today. On this Wednesday morning she was up first, long before her alarm rang.

Today was the play-off game against Longhorn Acres Middle School. Ashland Middle School had to win to get into the state semifinals. Ava was fired up and ready to win.

She touched her toes, then dropped down

for ten push-ups. She stretched her legs, loosening her muscles for the big kick. She played kicker. She was determined to make every extra point at today's game.

She kicked one of her jerseys off the floor. It arched up and landed atop another pile of clothes. Ava's messy room made Alex crazy. Unlike Ava, Alex was always so neat and orderly.

She scooped up the jersey nearest her and was about to pull it over her head when she remembered that the play-off was an away game. She groaned.

Ava had always loved football. She'd diagrammed plays in her coloring books when she was little. She'd slept holding a football instead of a stuffed animal.

But the only thing she hated about being part of the school football team was the away-game tradition. The entire team had to dress in their best clothes for school on game day.

For the boys, that meant suits and ties. For her, that meant a skirt, a nice shirt, and real shoes.

It was one thing to get dressed up for church and dinner at her grandma Beth's house, but another to have to sit in class in a skirt. Ava supposed it showed respect, but she still hated it.

She opened her closet. Her denim miniskirt hung where her mother had put it after the last away-game day. It was her go-to skirt. It was the only one that wasn't itchy.

Ava pulled it on. *What do I wear on top?* she wondered. The boys didn't have this problem. Every week they wore the same suit and tie, as if it were a uniform too. Ava was envious.

In a back corner, she spotted a purple short-sleeved sweater. She vaguely remembered her mother bringing it home from a shopping trip when they first moved. She examined it. The tags were still on, and the material felt soft. Ava pulled it over her head and ripped off the tags.

She could hear Coach and Tommy moving around now. She rummaged in her backpack for the printout of plays for today's game. She'd been over them so many times, but she wanted to be extra sure she knew them.

A knock sounded on her door, and her dad peeked his head in. His dark hair was covered by a Tigers cap. "I thought I was still dreaming when I saw your light on," he teased. "Game day jitters?"

Ava shook her head. "Game day excitement."

"That's my girl!" Coach beamed proudly.

"Tommy and I are going in early to watch film. The Rutland Raiders have a tricky running back. We need to figure out his moves."

"Look who's up early!" Mrs. Sackett called, stepping into Ava's room.

"You guys act like it's a big deal," Ava said. "Look behind you. That's a big deal."

Her parents turned, and the three of them stared at Tommy. His button-down shirt was wrinkle free and tucked into a pair of ironed khakis. His curly hair was styled with what looked to Ava to be gel, and she'd smelled his cologne long before she saw him.

Mrs. Sackett squinted at her son. "What's with the snazzy outfit?"

"Nothing," Tommy said.

"Tommy has a girlfriend!" Ava sang out. "He's trying to impress Cassie."

"She's your *girlfriend*?" Mrs. Sackett sounded surprised. "I thought she was just a Homecoming date."

"She's not my girlfriend. We don't do labels like that." He turned away, but Ava saw the blush creep up his neck.

"Tommy likes her," Ava mouthed to her parents. She liked Cassie too. The one time she'd met her, Cassie had been wearing a Patriots jersey. If Tommy was going to get all crazy about a girl, at least it was one who not only liked football but also liked the Patriots.

Coach frowned. "Tom, this isn't the time. Everything is riding on our game this weekend. I need your attention on the field. Not on some girl—"

"Thanks a lot, Ava," Tommy called, heading down the stairs.

"Sorry," Ava said. She knew it was hard for Tom to have their dad as his coach. He never got a break. "Hey, I'll catch a ride with you guys now, okay? I want to get to school early too."

She figured that was the least she could do for Tommy. Coach would talk to her about the upcoming game, and Tommy would get to just stare out the window and listen to his music.

As it turned out, no one talked in the car. Instead they listened to the local radio station's sports show. Two announcers who said they were reviewing her dad's coaching strategy managed to criticize everything he had done so far this season.

"Oh, please!" Ava cried. "Your team is winning. What are they moaning about?"

"Everyone in this town thinks they're a better coach," Tommy quipped. "The lunch ladies. The bagger in the grocery store. The crossing guards. You should hear them all go on."

"You're doing a great job," Ava told Coach. "This is dumb." She reached to turn off the radio.

"No!" Coach stopped her. "Leave it on."

"Can Coach Sackett bring in the big win?" one announcer asked. "All the games up until now were child's play. It's all about the big win."

The other announcer made a disapproving *tsk-tsk* noise. "A big win needs big experience. Coach Sackett doesn't have the track record. I fear he doesn't have the nerves for this level of football."

They listened in silence as the announcers second-guessed every decision he'd made all year.

Coach shook his head. "They should try getting out from behind their microphone and onto the field. Then we'll see who has the nerves for this game."

Ava grinned. "You tell them!" If anyone knew how to best guide a team to victory, it was Coach. Ava wished everyone would stop questioning him.

Five minutes later, she stepped out onto the sidewalk in front of the middle school. The toxic radio show continued to blare out the car window as she watched her dad drive down the shared driveway toward the high school.

"Is everything okay?" asked a girl behind her.

Ava turned to find Charlotte standing there. Her long brown hair was piled into a messy bun, and she wore a cute tank dress and black ankle boots. Picking out an outfit obviously came easily to her.

"Fine." Ava wriggled uncomfortably in her skirt. She didn't know how to feel about Charlotte after what had happened Monday at lunch.

"You don't look fine," Charlotte said. "You look upset."

"It's my dad," Ava explained. "The big high school game is on Saturday. If they win, they're on the path to the state tournament. He's supposed get Ashland the big win. That's what they called it on the radio."

"Can he?" Charlotte asked.

Ava shrugged. "He's an amazing coach. But the Rutland Raiders—that's who they're playing—are a great team. Everything is riding on this. I mean, this is why we moved here. His birthday is on Sunday, and we can't even talk about it, because he's too stressed. He hasn't baked anything in weeks."

"And that's weird?" Charlotte asked.

"Yes. Coach loves to bake. Cookies and muffins, especially," Ava explained. "But his complete focus is on the game and nothing else."

"Don't you have a game today too?" Charlotte asked.

Ava raised her eyebrows. She was surprised that Charlotte knew this. They had barely seen each other since Monday. "I do. But I'm sure I can make the field goals if they aren't crazy far."

"To be honest, I have no idea what a field goal is. I'm thinking it's a good thing. Perhaps better than barbecue?" Charlotte smiled.

"Definitely better." Ava gave a slight smile. Then she frowned. "It's horrible seeing Coach this tense."

"A party is the answer," Charlotte said. "And chocolate. Always chocolate."

"He said no parties," Ava reported.

"So how about just a family meal with all his favorite foods?" Charlotte asked.

Ava laughed. "Coach does love breakfast foods. French toast with powdered sugar, omelets, biscuits."

"Have you ever had chocolate-covered bacon? It's crazy good. There's a restaurant in New York that sells it. You could make him that," Charlotte suggested. "Chocolate plus breakfast. Pretty perfect, huh?"

"True," Ava said, grateful to Charlotte for helping her come up with ideas. Then she shook her head. "But he won't agree to it."

"Make it a surprise for Sunday morning," Charlotte said. "If he wins, he's happy. If he loses, you have this amazing breakfast to cheer him up. I mean, who wouldn't be cheered up by chocolate-covered bacon?"

"I like the way you think," said Ava, following Charlotte into the school.

For a moment, she thought of asking Charlotte what had happened at lunch on Monday, but decided to let it pass. Charlotte had probably been nervous on her first day. Ava had said plenty of stupid things herself in the past. Charlotte was nice, fun—and she was obviously going to be a good friend.

That, Ava decided, *is all that I need to know.*

The front door slammed, jolting Alex awake. She blinked several times, her eyes slowly adjusting to the sunlight streaming through the gaps in her shades.

Then she heard Moxy whimper from all the way downstairs.

"Oh no!" Alex bolted upright. She knew what that sound meant. Her dad had left for school already. Moxy always cried when Coach left.

"It's not really this late, is it?" She stared in horror at her bedside clock. She didn't remember turning off her alarm. She gazed at her laptop, open on her desk. The windows on the screen were still open to the pages on psychic abilities in twins. She'd stayed up late reading.

"Alex? You up?" Mrs. Sackett called upstairs. "Ava left with Daddy and Tommy. Get dressed fast and you can still make the bus. I'll wrap a muffin for you. Hurry!"

Alex swung her legs onto the floor and ran to her closet.

She didn't do last-minute well. She liked to pick out the perfect outfit the night before. But last night she hadn't been able to pull herself away from the screen.

She'd discovered that the better word to

describe her and Ava was telepathic, not psychic. Psychic was too general a term. Telepathic meant two people could send information back and forth using only their minds.

A famous psychic researcher she'd read about reported that only 30 percent of all identical twins shared telepathic abilities. Were she and Ava part of that 30 percent? She couldn't be sure. She'd taken several online quizzes, but the results were all over the place. Some telepathic twins reported never having to use words to talk with each other. They could just send messages with their minds. Was that what had happened at lunch on Monday? But then why didn't Ava send her a telepathic message that she was leaving early? Didn't she know that Alex had wanted to go in early today too?

"Alex, watch the clock!" her mom called.

Alex reached into her closet and grabbed the first top and bottom she touched. She sprinted to the bathroom, washed up, pulled her hair into a ponytail, and made it to the end of the block, muffin in hand, as the bus pulled up.

She kept her head down, reviewing the study guide she'd made for the social studies quiz today. She wondered if Ava had reviewed for her quiz this morning. Probably not. If Ava reviewed anything, it was her football plays. She and Ava were so different when it came to school.

When it came to clothes.

When it came to a lot of things.

Alex walked through the school halls toward her locker, her eyes still on her notes. She'd written each event on her Industrial Revolution time line in a different color. It made the study guide look pretty. And she liked pretty.

"Double trouble today, Alex!" Jack called loudly.

She looked up. "What?"

"Oops, I saw her again!" Logan Medina elbowed Jack. The two boys cracked up as the bell rang. They ran down the hall.

Alex shrugged. Boys were weird. She slipped into her seat in her homeroom.

"Ooh! Twice as nice," Lindsey whispered across the aisle.

Alex wrinkled her nose. "Huh?"

"The whole matching thing," Lindsey said. "Did you plan it?"

"Girls!" Mr. Kenerson called from the front of the room. "Listen up."

As Mrs. Gusman read the list of after-school

clubs over the crackly loudspeaker, Alex wondered what Lindsey was talking about. *Did I plan* what?

Before she could ask, the bell rang again, and Lindsey shot out the door to her first class, mouthing apologetically to Alex that she needed to study before her English quiz.

Alex headed down the opposite hall to science. Her mind snapped to the lab they were working on.

Slowly she became aware of the whispers.

And a giggle. A snicker. Another giggle.

She glanced to the sides of the hall. People were watching her.

Why? What's wrong? Her palms began to sweat. She tugged at her skirt.

Another snicker. She raised her head.

"Oh, wow." Her words came out in a whisper. She stared, her mouth hanging open.

Walking toward her was . . . *her!*

Same light-purple V-neck sweater. Same denim skirt. Same black flats. And the same face.

But it's not, Alex suddenly realized. *Not exactly.*

"Ava!" she cried.

Ava hurried toward her, ignoring all the kids who had stopped to watch. Her familiar laughter spilled out in gasps. "Seriously, Alex? This is hysterical! Look at us."

"W-why are you dressed like that? Like me?" Alex sputtered.

"I have an away game today, so I had to dress up," Ava explained. "What are the chances? We haven't done the matchy-matchy thing since those frilly yellow Easter dresses Mom made us wear when we were six. Remember? We looked like Peeps."

What *were* the chances? Alex wondered. Her sister wore jerseys to school. Always.

"How did you choose that outfit?" She squinted at her twin. She didn't even know they owned the same sweater.

Ava shrugged. "No real thought. I just grabbed what called to me. What about you?"

"Same," Alex admitted. "Except—"

Goose bumps prickled her arms as the realization hit her. This was the proof she'd been looking for. "Do you know what this means, Ave?"

"That we can't be seen together today?" Ava asked.

"No, it means we sent each other messages with our minds, and we wore matching outfits!" Alex cried. "We *do* have psychic abilities!"

CHAPTER FIVE

"Is this a thing here? Do you and your sister dress the same a lot?" Charlotte asked Ava outside the cafeteria. She'd caught up with Ava in the hallway, and Ava had invited her to sit with her and Kylie again. Charlotte had missed lunch yesterday to take a placement test for math.

"So not a thing," Ava said. When she'd first spotted Alex, she'd found it funny. Then everyone kept asking about it. She was self-conscious enough in a skirt without the school weighing in on their matching outfits.

"I didn't think so," Charlotte said, walking through the cafeteria doors. "You two don't seem to have the same style. Alex is in my English class."

"Whoa!" Ava reached out to stop Charlotte. "Kylie's sitting next to Owen. Aren't they really cute together?"

They watched Kylie show Owen something in a notebook. Owen smiled, then darted his eyes around. He spotted Logan and Corey headed his way. He stiffened and inched away. Kylie hesitated, then rose from her seat, as if to leave.

"Oh, no! We can't let her go," Ava said. "We need to get over there."

"There?" Charlotte sounded unsure.

"Yes! Follow me." Ava hurried across the cafeteria with Charlotte a few paces behind.

"Hey there." She plopped her brown lunch bag on the table. "Did you guys buy or bring today? Owen, you met Charlotte, right? Okay if we sit here? I want Charlotte to get to know as many kids as possible. I'm her student ambassador. Got to do my job!" Ava was babbling, but she had to keep Kylie next to Owen. She sat on one side of Kylie. Kylie shot her a grateful grin.

She got Owen talking about the book she knew that he and Kylie liked. She'd never read it. Owen was pretty shy, but Kylie jumped right in. Soon they were talking again, and Owen didn't seem to care that his buddies had sat down.

"Charlotte, sit here." Ava had just noticed Charlotte hovering by the table. She patted the seat next to her, and Charlotte perched on it, looking ready to bolt at any minute.

Lindsey, Emily, and Rosa made their way to the table.

"Where's Alex?" Ava asked Emily.

"She had to do something for student council," Emily said, sliding across from Ava. "She'll be late."

"Are you and Alex wearing the same outfits to my party, too?" Lindsey asked Ava, sizing up the sweater-skirt combo. "Matching costumes could be cute."

"I'm pretty certain that today is our first and last identical appearance at Ashland Middle School," Ava said.

"Hey, Lindz, we could match. And so could Rosa and Annelise. Matching could be the costume theme," Emily said.

"It's already the theme here," Charlotte muttered. Everyone gazed at Lindsey, Emily, and Rosa's blue-and-white cheerleader outfits. They were cheering at the game tonight, so they'd come to school in uniform.

"Do you cheer?" Emily asked Charlotte, ignoring her sneer.

"Please." Charlotte snorted. "I do ballet."

"What's that supposed to mean?" Rosa asked, crossing her arms. "Cheerleading is so much harder than ballet."

"For real?" Charlotte screwed up her nose. "Have you ever tried a grand jeté or a pirouette?"

"Have you ever tried a full layout twist or a basket toss?" Rosa retorted.

"Both cheerleading and ballet are athletic and hard," Ava piped up, trying to ease the sudden tension. "I'd look deranged if I tried either," she joked, even though it wasn't true—she was pretty coordinated.

"That could be a funny costume," Charlotte said. "I'll be a deranged Texas cheerleader for Halloween."

"What?" Lindsey asked, eyebrows raised.

"I'm thinking a blond wig, cheering outfit, cowboy boots, cowboy hat, and a rodeo lasso." Charlotte laughed.

But no one else did.

"Hey, it was a joke." Charlotte raised her arms in mock surrender.

"Fine, but you can only come to my party if you wear a different costume," Lindsey said. "Nothing with cheerleading."

"Last year my friends and I all dressed as 1920s flappers. I wore a vintage teal fringe dress. Ah-mah-zing," Charlotte said. "But I won't be making an appearance at your party. I don't do hoedowns."

"What are you talking about?" Lindsey cried.

"You guys square dance at parties, right?" Charlotte asked.

"No one here square dances," Emily replied tightly.

"Actually, they made us square dance in gym last year," Logan offered. Lindsey glared at him.

Ava looked over at Kylie, but she was still talking to Owen about the book. She hadn't even heard the awkward conversation.

Why is Charlotte acting so mean? Ava wondered, feeling uncomfortable. She couldn't figure it out. Did she not like Lindsey, Emily, and Rosa?

"You know, Ashland is a really cool place. You should give it a chance," Lindsey said.

Ava was amazed that Lindsey was still talking to Charlotte, and even more amazed that she was still trying to be nice.

Ava opened her eyes wide at Charlotte, trying to signal her to back off. But Charlotte didn't take the hint.

"Is that one of your little cheers? Rah, rah, go Texas?" Charlotte asked sarcastically.

Lindsey gave Emily a disgusted look. Then they both glanced at Ava, as if Charlotte's rudeness were her fault.

"Let's go throw out our trash," Emily said abruptly.

"Definitely," said Lindsey. She and Rosa followed Emily away from the table. They whispered as they walked.

Ava knew they were talking about Charlotte. She wanted to tell them that Charlotte wasn't like this. That she'd been so nice to Ava this morning. But she didn't run after them. Because what did she really know about Charlotte? She usually was a pretty good judge of people. But Charlotte totally confused her.

Alex focused all her attention on the purple gel pen on the kitchen table.

The pen. Think about the pen. Nothing but the gel pen, she told herself.

She stared at it with laser vision. Keeping her body completely still, she coaxed her mind to transfer energy into the pen, to send her life force into the pen.

She pressed her palms together, as if in yoga class.

The mosquito bite behind her knee itched.

She ignored it. She had to use her telepathic powers to make the pen write. Or float. Or move. Or something.

She squeezed her eyes tightly, willing the pen into motion.

But the pen just lay there. Motionless.

Alex blew out a huge breath. And even that didn't move the gel pen.

She chewed her lip, contemplating what she was doing wrong. Sibyl's website said people with the Power could move objects. And it was only a pen. It wasn't an elephant.

Maybe I need Ava, she thought. Sibyl had said something about their Power being stronger together. Now she wished she'd listened more closely. She also wished she'd bought the psychic's book. After all the research she'd done, she was now convinced that Sibyl wasn't a fake.

She was also convinced that she and Ava shared some kind of power, or connection, or psychic wavelength. More than the "twin-speak" her dad liked to joke about. She wished Ava were here to try moving the pen with her.

At that moment, her phone buzzed, startling her. Could it be Ava? Had Alex mentally summoned her again?

Alex looked at the screen. No. It was a text from Charlotte Huang, the new girl.

Wanna come to my house Friday
after school? U & Ava. It'll be fun.
Just the 3 of us. Cool?

Cool! We are in!

She'd only really spoken to Charlotte this afternoon. They had English together and were paired up on a grammar activity. They'd spent more time talking about fashion and jewelry than diagramming sentences. Alex loved Charlotte's sense of style. And Charlotte had complimented Alex's silver bead necklace. She seemed to think that Alex would fit in living in New York City. How amazing was that?

"We're home!" Mrs. Sackett announced, pushing open the kitchen door.

Moxy bounded down the steps from where she'd been asleep in the upstairs hallway. She rushed to greet Mrs. Sackett.

Alex craned her neck to see over her mom's shoulder. Ava still wore her football uniform, minus the pads. Her curls were sweaty and matted to the sides of her face. A film of dirt coated her skin, and she smelled awful. But she was smiling.

"You won!" Alex leaped off her chair.

"We did! Twenty-one to sixteen!" Ava cheered. "We're moving on!"

Alex slapped her sister a high five. "I wish I'd been there. I can't believe Ms. Palmer scheduled an extra student council meeting this week. Were you awesome?"

Ava shrugged. "Pretty awesome. Three field goals."

Mrs. Sackett petted Moxy and surveyed the kitchen. "Alex? What about starting dinner? Didn't you get my text?"

"I set the table and put water in the pot for pasta," Alex said.

"What about making the salad?"

"Yeah, that. I meant to do it, but I was trying to move this pen with my mind," she explained.

"I don't even know what that means." Mrs. Sackett began pulling lettuce and cucumbers out of the fridge.

"How'd that work for you?" Ava smirked, plopping into a chair. She rolled the pen with her finger.

"It takes practice. I think we need to do it together," Alex said.

"Right now, you need to wash and cut theses veggies," her mom said. "I'm going to take Moxy out." She clipped a leash on the dog. "Ava, you need to shower."

"I'm too tired to move," Ava complained.

As Alex walked to the sink, she told Ava about Charlotte's invite. "I can't wait to see her closet. She brought all these cool clothes from New York City. We're all about the same size. She said we can share them," Alex reported.

"I don't want to share her clothes," Ava said.

"I bet she has other fun things for us to do." Alex scrubbed the cucumber with the vegetable brush.

"I don't want to go," Ava said.

"Why not? She seems so sweet," Alex said.

"No, she doesn't. At least, not all the time. I can't figure her out." Ava told Alex about how Charlotte had acted at the lunch table.

"You guys must not have understood her jokes. I'm sure it didn't go down like that."

"I was there. It was bad," Ava insisted.

"Emily and Lindsey just don't know her. Maybe they're intimidated, because she's sophisticated and from New York. I think we should go," Alex declared. "She wanted it to be the three of us."

Ava shrugged. "I'll give her another chance. But something is odd with her."

Alex pulled the wooden cutting board from the cabinet. Then she spotted the shopping bags on the floor. "You and Mom went shopping? Without me?"

"Don't get all jealous. We stopped at the mall, so I could get Coach a birthday present. Nothing else," Ava assured her.

"What did you get?" Alex asked.

"The most amazing gift ever." Ava stood and reached into the bag. She pulled out a football-shaped spatula. "He can use this to flip pancakes. Or burgers."

"Oh, I don't think he'll have to choose." Alex raced to her hiding place in the laundry room and returned holding her football-shaped spatula. "He can use one for pancakes and the other for burgers."

"You didn't!" Ava cried. "You got him the same one."

Alex nodded. She stared at the twin spatulas for a moment. True, it was the perfect gift, but . . . still . . .

"We're psychic, Ave," she said in a low voice.

Ava snorted. "Matching spatulas do not make us psychic."

"It's more than that. Much more." Alex sat beside her sister. "I didn't believe at first, but the evidence is there. All these sites talk about telepathic abilities in twins. And all this stuff has been happening lately. Reading each other's minds, wearing the same outfit, picking out this present. I feel it. Don't you?"

"I feel tired. And sweaty. And hungry," Ava admitted. "I don't feel psychic."

"You just need to give it a chance," Alex encouraged her. "Madame Sibyl says our Power is stronger together. We have to tune in to each other."

"So let me get this straight," Ava said. "I have a math test tomorrow. You're saying I can skip studying tonight, and if I think hard enough, you'll be able to mentally send me all the correct answers?"

Alex laughed. "Nice try. I don't think it works that way. And even if it did, I'm not doing it. We should use our Power for good."

"Acing my math test would be using it for good!" Ava protested.

"No, I mean it. I think we could do good things," Alex insisted.

"Like what?" Ava asked, as their mom opened the door and Moxy ran for her water bowl.

Alex scooted back to the cutting board. "I don't know yet. First, you have to be open to the idea. Are you?"

Ava pulled the cap off the gel pen. She scribbled on a paper napkin, then held it up. *NO!*

Alex sighed. She felt the Power. She really did! As she continued chopping, she focused her energies on Ava. They needed to be united to make it work. To do good and important things.

She *needed* to make her sister believe.

CHAPTER SIX

Alex rested Emily's signed copy of *The Power* on her lap on Friday afternoon.

"Do not get any food on it," Emily warned.

"Promise." Alex carefully speared with a toothpick the mini cubes of orange cheese her mom had packed for lunch. Mrs. Sackett's lunches were so much worse than Coach's. But Coach hadn't been around this week. He was on the field or in his office tucked inside the high school locker room, completely focused on the big game. He hadn't even had time to make her favorite hummus-and-vegetable wrap.

As everyone at the lunch table talked about Lindsey's party, Alex flipped through Sibyl's book. Yesterday she'd begged Emily to bring it to school. As she skimmed the pages, she decided that it wasn't half-bad. Sibyl described so many feelings that Alex had also had. The more she read, the more Alex was sure she could do psychic things.

They could do them. She needed Ava in this.

She raised her eyes and found Ava across the lunchroom, eating with Kylie. Charlotte wasn't there.

I'll talk to Ava tonight, she decided. *I'll go to the park and shoot baskets if that's what it takes to get her to try to move the pen with me.*

Alex knew she was getting a bit obsessed. She got this way about things. She'd hear about something that interested her, and then she'd research it to death on the Internet. She'd make charts and graphs of her new knowledge. She'd compare prices or reviews or whatever was important. She'd think about it nonstop until the next thing came along.

And now, all she could think about was the Power.

"Guys! Guys!" Rosa hurried over to the table. Her eyes were red and puffy, and Alex was sure she'd been crying. "Have any of you seen it? It's silver. You know it, right? Did you? Did you see it?" Her words tumbled out in between sobs.

"Whoa, Rosa, sit down." Lindsey guided her onto the bench. "What happened?"

"It's lost. Or stolen," she choked out. Her shoulders trembled.

"Ro, you're not making sense," Emily said.

"Take a deep breath," Alex offered. That was what her mom always told her.

Rosa sucked in some air. "My bracelet. The silver one I always wear," she began.

"The one you got for your confirmation?" Lindsey asked.

"Yes, that one. My parents gave it to me. It's really special. My mom got it from her mom when she was confirmed in Mexico," Rosa explained. "I wore it to school today. I'm totally sure of it. But now it's gone!" Tears welled up again in her big brown eyes.

"Did you look for it?" Corey asked.

"Of course I looked for it. I've looked everywhere," Rosa said. "I've covered the whole school."

"Well, where's the last place you saw it?" Xander asked.

"If I knew that, I'd know where it was!" Rosa

snapped. Then she dropped her head into her hands. "Sorry. I'm just so scared. I can't tell my mom I lost it."

"Don't worry. We'll help you look for it," Lindsey said, wrapping her arm around Rosa's shoulder.

"And Alex can use her Power," Emily put in.

Alex gulped. What was Emily suggesting?

"What's she going to do?" Lindsey asked, wrinkling her nose.

"You know how on the news you always hear about psychics finding lost pets?" Emily said.

"Not really," Xander said, smearing cream cheese on a bagel with his fingers.

Emily rolled her eyes at him. "Well, they do. All the time. Psychics find things that the police can't find. They use their minds and their powers. They conjure up an image of the missing thing. They can see *exactly* where it is," Emily reported, as if she were an expert on psychic treasure hunting.

"Really?" Rosa's dark eyes grew wide and hopeful. "Can you do that, Alex?"

Alex's stomach tightened. The cheese cube she'd just eaten lodged in her throat like a stone.

"Of course she can," Emily answered for her. "She and Ava have psychic powers."

Alex shook her head. "I don't think—"

"Oh, come on, Alex. You heard what Madame Sibyl said. And then you willed Ava to come over here, and you mentally told each other to wear the same outfit," Emily said.

"I know, but—" Before Alex could explain that she couldn't make a pen move yet, and she was still trying to convince her sister to try to even use her powers, Rosa flung her willowy arms around her and gave her a hug.

"If you could find my bracelet, Alex, I would be so grateful. I mean it. I need you to try. Please!" Rosa cried.

Alex awkwardly patted Rosa's back as the stone in her throat expanded.

Rosa pulled away. "So?"

Can Ava and I really do this? Alex wondered, unsure how to respond. Once more, all eyes were on her.

"You can do this," Emily said, as if she were the one who read minds. "I know you can."

"It would be so good if you found Rosa's bracelet," Lindsey added.

This is the good thing! Alex realized. *This is how we can use our Power for good.*

"Sure," she told Rosa. "We'll help you."

Rosa grinned and hugged her again. Alex had never felt very close to Rosa, but from how tight her hug was, Alex could tell how much she wanted this to work. "Will you do it now? Picture where it is and all?"

Alex glanced across the room at Ava, who was showing Kylie something in a book. Strangely, she felt more confident that she could find Rosa's bracelet than convince Ava to do it with her.

Ava rested her chin on her hands and listened to Kylie.

"The book is about teamwork. They're called the Souls, so even though they sound separate, they do come together," Kylie explained.

"In the academic bowl at the end, right?" Ava asked.

"Exactly!" Kylie grinned. "You're going to kill it on the in-class essay."

Ava had finished the book for English class last night and she understood it, but she'd had Kylie retell the story. Kylie made the plots and themes so much easier to understand. Plus, she did great voices and accents.

"You should be a teacher," Ava told her. "Or an actress."

"I could teach acting. Or act like I'm teaching," Kylie teased.

"Or you could—" Ava began.

"Ava, I need you." Alex had appeared behind her.

"What's wrong?" Ava asked, swiveling to see her better. Alex chewed her lip.

"It's kind of private." Alex glanced at Kylie.

"Are you okay? You can tell Kylie, too," Ava said.

"I need you. Alone," Alex urged. She shrugged at Kylie. "Sorry, but—"

"No worries. I can take the hint. I'm going to find Mr. Antonucci for extra social studies help." Kylie stood.

Ava waved and turned to Alex. "What's going on?" she demanded.

Alex eyed a table of boys nearby and Mr. Fifer, the music teacher, patrolling for trash. "Come to the bathroom with me." She tugged Ava's hand.

"You're scaring me," Ava said, following Alex to the girls' bathroom. They bypassed the one nearest the cafeteria. Instead Alex dragged her to the one all the way by the library. Once inside,

Alex peered underneath each stall, making sure they were truly alone.

"Okay, now I'm petrified," Ava admitted, leaning against a sink. "Are you in trouble? What happened?"

"Rosa lost her silver bracelet," Alex said.

"And?" Ava couldn't believe they were hidden away because of a bracelet. "Did you take it?"

"Of course not! But we're going to find it."

"I'm still not getting this. You want me to help you look for Rosa's bracelet?" Ava asked. The sink dripped behind her. The gray tile smelled of cleaning supplies.

"You and me. Together. With our Power," Alex said quietly. "Like we do when we read minds."

"We don't read minds," Ava scoffed. She couldn't believe her sister was getting so hung up on this stuff. Alex was usually the logical one.

"I think we can." Alex gave her a really intense look. "I promised Rosa we'd try. That together we could see where her missing bracelet is."

Ava blew out her breath. "We could just look around the school."

"She did that. Listen, Ave, everyone is counting on us to do this. And I really think we can. This is the good thing I was telling you about,"

Alex explained. "This bracelet is important to Rosa. You kind of owe it to her to try."

"The bell's going to ring in a few minutes," Ava said. This whole idea was too weird.

"We'll try really quickly. Come in here." Alex pulled Ava with her into a narrow stall. They squeezed on either side of the toilet. "I think it will work better if we're really close together."

"It stinks in here, Al." Ava felt silly standing with her sister in a stall. "What if someone walks in?"

"They'll think it's a twin thing," Alex replied.

"Going to the bathroom together? Oh, that's great." Ava blew out her breath. Then she sucked it back in. It really did stink.

Alex grasped both of Ava's hands over the toilet. "Close your eyes."

Ava closed her eyes. "You owe me big-time."

"Shhh. Now think about Rosa's bracelet. It's silver. It used to belong to her mother when she was a girl," Alex said.

Ava thought about a bracelet. She had no idea what Rosa's looked like exactly. "Is it working?"

"It doesn't happen that fast," Alex said. "Really concentrate on the bracelet. I will too. And try to form a picture in your mind of where it is right now."

The squeak of hinges alerted them to the opening of the bathroom door. Ava's eyes shot open. Alex motioned frantically to the toilet.

"What?" Ava mouthed.

"Get up!" Alex pointed to the sides of the toilet seat. School toilets had no lid.

Ava groaned. Gross! Then she heard the footsteps. And voices she didn't recognize. Ava leaped onto the toilet seat. Her sneakers balanced on either side of the bowl.

She tried not to look down.

Tried not to think about falling into toilet water.

Alex kept a grip on both her hands. Ava felt ridiculous. If any of those girls opened the stall door, what would they possibly think? She looked as if she were doing a circus routine!

"Is that a new lip gloss?" one girl asked. She sounded as if she were over by the mirrors.

"Yep. Super-sparkle shine. And it smells like grapefruit," said another.

Alex gave her hand a hard squeeze. "Think about the bracelet," she mouthed.

Ava tried. She really did.

The lip gloss girls left, and a pair of scuffed navy flats walked in. The girl headed toward the farthest stall.

Bracelet, Ava reminded herself. How long would she have to stay perched on a toilet? She heard the girl using the toilet. Ava stared with disgust into the toilet water below.

"Anything?" Alex mouthed.

Ava shook her head. Alex frowned.

They listened to the sink water run and the whir of the hand dryer. The girl left.

Ava hopped down. "I'm out of here, Alex. I tried. I really did."

"This wasn't a good place to do it," Alex conceded.

"Oh, you think?" Ava couldn't help being sarcastic. Then she caught sight of Alex's distraught face. "Look, I'm sorry it didn't work."

"I know it can, though. I think the two of us should focus on the bracelet all day. In all our classes. Even if we're not together physically, we can connect mentally. Will you try to access the Power today? Try to find the bracelet?" Alex sounded so desperate. Ava rarely heard her like this.

"Sure. Whatever," Ava agreed, hoping to make Alex happy. "But why are you so into this psychic stuff?"

Alex shrugged. The bell rang and they pushed

their way through the now-crowded hall. "Don't you ever wonder about the mind and how it works? Especially our minds and our connection? I want to test it out."

"It's so like you to be using us as a science experiment," Ava teased.

"Yeah, and it's more than that," Alex admitted. "I kind of told everyone we could do it."

Ava stopped walking. Sometimes she thought Alex would say anything when faced with a crowd. "This is going to end badly," she warned.

"You don't know that," Alex countered. "Think positive thoughts. We can access the Power together."

Ava nodded, but she didn't feel very positive. She could barely remember the plot to the book she had to write an essay on in two minutes. How was she going to conjure up a missing bracelet with her mind?

CHAPTER SEVEN

Alex spent the afternoon thinking about Rosa's bracelet.

Her head was starting to pound. She had no idea where it was.

In English class, she waited until Charlotte walked to the front of the room to get their discussion questions. Then she closed her eyes and tried again.

Rosa's bracelet. Rosa's bracelet.

She smelled freshly baked cookies. Was that a clue? Maybe the bracelet was in the cafeteria kitchen! Maybe Rosa had accidentally left it on her tray when she turned it in. *But do they actually bake the cookies in the cafeteria?* Alex wondered.

"Alex? Are you asleep?" Charlotte whispered.

Alex blinked. "No, just thinking." Then she noticed the plate with two cookies that Charlotte was holding. "What's that?"

"Ms. Palmer brought in cookies today and said we could each have one." Charlotte passed Alex a cookie and the paper with their discussion questions.

Alex inhaled the buttery scent of the treats. Great. She was no closer to finding Rosa's bracelet. "Okay, let's do this." She started looking over the questions, but she really didn't feel like talking about *Animal Farm* right now, and she could tell Charlotte didn't either.

"I had to take another placement test during lunch. That was *not* fun," Charlotte said. "You and Ava are still coming over today?"

"Definitely," Alex said. "Ava has football practice and I have to help the cheerleaders, but we can come over after."

Charlotte raised her eyebrows. "I didn't think you were one of them."

"Them?" Alex thumbed through the book when she noticed Ms. Palmer watching them.

"The cheerleaders," Charlotte said.

"I'm not. I wanted to be, but I'm way too

uncoordinated. You should see the crazy-hard flips they do. So I help them with fund-raising and advertising," Alex explained.

Charlotte raised her eyebrows but didn't say anything. "So after that, we'll hang out? I live right nearby. I can meet you at the front of the school."

Alex took a bite of cookie and chewed thoughtfully. She also wanted to grab Ava and try calling up the whereabouts of the bracelet again, and she thought it made sense to do that on school grounds, where the bracelet was lost. But if she intercepted Ava as she came out of the locker room, they could try before meeting Charlotte.

"We're good, right?" Charlotte sounded nervous.

"All good," Alex assured her, glancing up at the clock. As soon as classes were over, she planned to hurry to the library. She wanted to check Madame Sibyl's site. Maybe they weren't doing it right. Maybe they shouldn't hold hands. Or maybe they needed to be in a dark room. She needed more information.

But the library doors were locked after school when she pulled on them. A handwritten sign on notebook paper said LIBRARY CLOSED FOR STAFF MEETING.

Alex wished she could pick up wireless Internet and search on her phone, but the school constantly changed the passwords so kids couldn't log on to the network.

She headed toward the gym. The cheerleaders' voices rang out as she opened the door: "One, three, five, nine, who do we think is mighty fine?"

"Did you find it? Say yes!" Rosa ran over to Alex before she'd stepped fully inside.

Emily, Lindsey, Annelise, and all the other cheerleaders gathered around. The air crackled with their anticipation.

"Not yet," Alex admitted. Her phone buzzed, but she ignored it. "I'm really trying."

"I am in *so* much trouble." Rosa groaned. "If I can sneak up to my room, maybe my mom won't notice. At least for today."

"Don't stress," Emily told Rosa. "I know Alex will find it."

Alex wondered how Emily was so sure. Emily was always the most optimistic of her group of friends, but still . . . the bracelet could be *anywhere*.

"Alex, let's talk posters," called Coach Jen,

as Alex's phone buzzed again. "Lindsey, I want you to lead the squad through the syncopation sequence. Slow it down. Hit every beat."

Some girls grumbled.

Coach Jen wagged a finger at them. "Don't give me that. At least we're in the air-conditioning. Remember how hot it was outside this morning before school?"

"Before school?" Alex asked.

Rosa nodded. "We're doing double practice sessions to get ready for the play-off games. We were on the field this morning."

As Coach Jen described the posters that she wanted Alex to make for their upcoming bake sale, Alex thought hard about Rosa's bracelet. Luckily, she was great at multitasking, so she still managed to write down the exact wording Coach Jen wanted.

The bracelet. The bracelet. Silver. Confirmation. Family heirloom.

She repeated the words, trying desperately to call up an image.

"So you'll make them look nice?" Coach Jen asked. "Alex? Alex?"

"What? Oh, yes, of course. I have great handwriting and these thick, colorful markers," Alex said. "I'll have them for you on Monday."

"Perfect," Coach Jen said before returning to the cheerleaders.

Alex finally pulled her phone from her pocket. Ava had been texting her.

Check the inside of R's gym locker door.

?????

Alex texted back. She waited. Ava didn't reply.

She must be on the football field, Alex realized.

Had Ava seen something? Alex was dying to know. She closed her eyes. She saw nothing.

She wandered into the girls' locker room. Walking up and down the aisles, she realized that the gray metal lockers all looked the same. She had no idea which was Rosa's. Plus, they were all locked.

Sweatshirts, shoes, and backpacks were piled

on the floor and the wooden benches.

Alex cleared some space and dropped onto a bench. Now what? She needed Rosa if she wanted to open her locker. She needed Ava to make the Power work. And she couldn't check Sibyl's site.

She had no choice. She sat on the bench and worked on her homework.

She heard their voices before she saw them. Lindsey's high-pitched voice rose above them all. "You *have* to come in a costume, Carly. I'm serious. I will not let you in without one!"

A costume! Alex thought, suddenly remembering that Halloween was only one day away. She was so not a last-minute girl. She needed to get moving on this, especially if she wasn't going to follow her original plan.

"Hey, Alex, you're still here." Emily sounded surprised.

"Just waiting for Ava to finish," Alex said, pushing her notebooks back into her backpack. "Rosa?"

Rosa turned expectantly. She rummaged in a purple plaid backpack leaning against a locker.

"This may sound weird, but can I look inside your locker?" Alex asked.

"Did you have a vision?" Emily said excitedly.

Alex shrugged. She wished she could've talked to Ava first. Maybe Ava's text had nothing to do with the bracelet. That would be bad.

"Sure." Rosa twisted the dial. Right. Left. Right.

Alex braced herself for major embarrassment.

Then Rosa lifted the latch and pulled open the door. Rosa and Emily peered into the locker. But Alex looked at the inside of the door.

"Your bracelet!" she cried. Her voice cracked with surprise.

All the girls crowded around, staring in amazement at the delicate silver bracelet dangling from a piece of metal protruding from the door.

Rosa's squeal pierced the shocked silence. "You did it! You're the best, Alex!"

Alex felt her face flush. There was the bracelet. Exactly where Ava had said it was.

A shiver traveled down her neck. She was excited and also a little afraid. Somehow, all that thinking about and focusing on the bracelet had worked. Ava had seen the bracelet.

We have the Power! We truly have the Power!

Alex wanted to dance. To jump. To scream.

"Happy to help," she said instead, as if she

tracked down missing items all the time. Rosa fastened her bracelet onto her wrist, while Emily gave Alex a big hug.

"That was amazing," Lindsey said. "I am truly in awe."

Alex grinned. Even though she hadn't lived in Ashland long, she knew impressing Lindsey was not easy. And with Lindsey came the rest of the girls. And a lot of the boys, too.

"Tell us how you did it," Annelise begged.

"Um, I will later," Alex promised. "I've got to meet Ava." She headed out of the locker room. She knew it was best to escape before she had to explain.

Because she had absolutely no idea how she and Ava had done it.

Ava jogged the final postpractice lap, keeping pace with Owen. Owen was one of the fastest on the team. Ava never liked to be far behind. The Texas sun beat down onto her neck, even though it was almost November. Back in Massachusetts, the air would be crisp and the leaves would be orange. Oddly, she didn't really miss it. Not the way she thought she would. She was getting used to the Texas heat.

"Good work!" Coach Kenerson slapped each player a high five, as he called an end to the practice. "We go to double sessions tomorrow. Seven o'clock on the turf. Special teams, I'm working with you first." He took a big swig from a bottle of iced tea. Ava eyed it longingly.

She gazed toward the bleachers where she'd left her now-lukewarm water bottle. She squinted into the sun. Alex, wearing a red eyelet sundress, stood on the bleachers. Her long hair fell past her shoulders, and her curls bounced as she waved eagerly to Ava.

Ava jogged over. Her own hair was sweaty and plastered to her neck. Her jersey was streaked with dirt where Xander had tackled her onto the ground. *We look like the before and after of a reality TV makeover show,* Ava decided. She shrugged. She'd much rather be in her filthy jersey than the strappy sandals Alex wore, which, Ava knew for a fact, left painful indentations on her feet.

"Why are you here?" Ava asked, reaching for her water bottle. Alex rarely watched practice.

"Just tell me how," Alex whispered. "How did you do it?"

"Do what?" Ava took a big gulp. Gross. It was totally warm.

Alex glanced around. The boys gathered their stuff and trudged, heads down, into the locker room. The sports bus would be here in ten minutes. When Alex seemed certain that no one was listening, she grabbed Ava by the shoulders. "It worked! We found the bracelet!"

"Really?" Ava draped a towel around her neck and turned toward the girls' locker room.

"Ave, stop. Did you hear me? Isn't it the best thing ever? We linked our minds and psychically found Rosa's bracelet!" Alex put her hands together in a flurry of excited claps.

"So the bracelet was in her locker?" Ava asked. She couldn't believe how happy Alex looked. It was as if she'd found a winning lottery ticket.

"Exactly where you told me it would be. Did you have a vision? I can't believe we can seriously do this. I mean, I can believe it. I knew we had the Power!" Alex's words came out at rapid-fire pace.

Ava didn't say anything. She began walking. Alex followed, beaming with happiness.

"Lindsey and Emily and everyone were so

impressed. No, not impressed. In awe. Stupefied. Astonished. Stunned." Alex wrinkled her nose. "Wait. I can think of more synonyms."

"I get it," Ava assured her.

"I knew we were special," Alex said.

Ava cleared her throat several times. She took another swig of the horrible water to buy time.

The truth was she'd stopped thinking about Rosa's bracelet the minute she hopped off the toilet seat. But when she'd gone into the girls' locker room to change for practice, the hair band she wore around her wrist caught on the tiny piece of metal jutting out from the slats on the inside of the locker. This happened a lot. Sometimes she didn't feel it and then found the hair band hanging there days later.

Then she thought about Rosa's bracelet and thought that maybe that was where it was. But the cheerleaders hadn't appeared in the locker room yet, so she'd texted Alex.

It had been a logical hunch.

It hadn't been the Power, or whatever Alex was calling it.

Alex, of all people, should appreciate how I used logic to solve the case of the missing brace-let, Ava thought. Her sister was the Queen of

Logic. Except now, when she wanted to believe in this twin power thing.

"So?" Alex pressed her.

"It's totally amazing," Ava agreed. "I'm happy for Rosa. Listen, you should find Charlotte. I'm sure she's waiting. I'll meet you guys out front in a minute." Before Alex could speak, Ava slipped into the locker room.

She leaned her back against the door, taking in the quiet, cavernous room. All the other girls who played sports had come and gone. Her heart beat loudly in the silence.

She knew she should've been honest with Alex. But she hadn't lied. Not really.

Tonight I'll tell her how I found the bracelet, Ava promised herself. *It'll be fine if Alex believes we're special.*

At least for a little while.

CHAPTER EIGHT

"Bendel, then Bloomie's, then Bergdorf and Barneys," Charlotte was saying to Alex when Ava found them in front of the school.

"What are you talking about?" Ava asked.

"Charlotte's ranking her favorite department stores in New York City," Alex explained.

"Oh." Ava hadn't heard of any of them. But right now, she'd rather talk shopping than psychic powers.

"The stores all start with *B*," Alex said to Charlotte.

Ava smiled. This was Alex's way of taking mental notes. She was big on memory tricks, such as remembering the first letter of something. Ava knew she'd find Alex on her computer tonight, researching each and every store.

Ava didn't care. If she ever visited New York City, there was no way she was going shopping. She hated department stores.

"My house is behind there." Charlotte pointed toward the row of tall trees lining the long driveway leading down to the high school. "If we cut through the back, it's a lot faster than walking to the road. And then we don't have to go through the gate."

"What gate?" Ava asked, following Alex and Charlotte across the school's front lawn.

"The gate to our neighborhood," Charlotte said.

Ava shot Alex a meaningful look. There were only a few gated communities in Ashland, and they all had big, fancy houses. The Sacketts lived on a small road with no gate.

"Are you going to Lindsey's party tomorrow?" Alex asked as they rounded the tree trunks.

"Are you?" Charlotte asked.

"Definitely," Alex said. "But I don't have a costume yet, and that's stressing me out."

"If I go—and I don't know that I will—we could all be something together. The three of us," Charlotte suggested. "Snap, Crackle, and Pop. Or the Three Bears."

"Count me out," Ava said. "I'm not doing anything that cutesy."

"Okay, what if we're East Coast baseball players?" Charlotte said. "The Yankees, the Mets, and the Red Sox. Those are the correct names, right?"

"That wouldn't be so bad," Ava conceded.

"That's not dressing up enough. The whole point of Halloween is lots of makeup, a costume, maybe even a wig," Alex protested. "Really go wild."

"My mom has a whole separate closet with all these crazy vintage clothes," Charlotte offered. They were cutting through a huge backyard with a massive swing set, a stone fire pit, a gleaming basketball court with regulation hoop, and manicured, bright-green grass. "I bet we'll find something in there."

"You live here?" Alex asked in awe, as they walked around to the sprawling front yard. The house was enormous. Two huge planters overflowing with purple flowers bordered an imposing dark-red front door.

"Seems so," Charlotte muttered. She jiggled a key in the lock and pushed open the door.

An icy blast hit Ava as she stepped into the stone tiled foyer. The air-conditioning was on full force. She could hear the faint whirring of its motor in the silent house.

"Wow! It's so big," Ava said, staring up at the tall ceilings and heavy iron chandelier. She didn't say it was also so quiet and cold. "Where is everyone?"

"Carmen went to pick up my little brother, Ben, at school. I think she took Harvey." Charlotte dropped her backpack on an antique-looking bench. Two large cardboard boxes rested alongside it.

"Who're Carmen and Harvey?" Ava asked.

Alex shot her a disapproving look.

Ava shrugged. Charlotte didn't have to answer if she didn't want to.

"Carmen is our babysitter. She's really more for Ben—I'm too old for that. And Harvey is our dog," Charlotte explained. "He's freaked out by all the nature out here. He hates to pee on the grass. He's used to sidewalks. Like me. I mean the sidewalks part, not the peeing part. He's always looking for concrete."

"We have a dog too," Alex said. "But Moxy loves to be outside. She falls asleep on the grass."

Ava wondered where Charlotte's parents were—and why she didn't mention them. But she didn't ask. If she did, Alex would probably give her another death stare.

"Want to see my room?" Charlotte led them up the stairs. Large boxes lined the hallways. Ava guessed they were still unpacking. Charlotte opened a door to an oversize bedroom, chicly decorated in black, white, and hot pink.

"I love it!" Alex squealed. "Are all these perfumes yours?"

Nearly fifty cut-glass bottles of various shapes, colors, and sizes crowded a sleek white vanity topped by an enormous mirror in an ornate hot-pink frame.

Charlotte nodded. "I love scents. We once went on vacation to the south of France, and I got to design my own signature scent. Want to smell it?"

"Please!" Alex positioned herself alongside Charlotte at the vanity. As Charlotte sprayed and dabbed perfume after perfume on the inside of her arm, different scents crowded the air. Floral. Citrus. Woodsy. One hung top of the other.

Ava's stomach churned. "I need air," she squeaked.

"Wait! Charlotte's going to show us all her lip

glosses. She has over one hundred! Her mom is a makeup executive. How cool is that?" Alex asked, her words running together.

Ava stepped over to the window. It was covered by a sheet of brown craft paper. Someone had taken a red marker and drawn a pattern of rectangles on it. They looked amazingly like real bricks.

"What's this?" she asked Charlotte.

"Keeping NYC in and Texas out," Charlotte declared. She began to say something else and then grimaced.

"You're a great artist." Ava stared at the fake wall, unsure what it meant exactly. The perfume cloud was making her eyes water. Ava peeled up the bottom flap of the paper, which hadn't been taped securely to the sill. Could she open the window and get some air?

Outside she spotted a thin, dark-haired boy shooting a basketball. Shooting it badly. The ball kept hitting the backboard. But that didn't matter. Ava knew this was the perfect excuse. "Is that your brother? Can I go check out your backyard?" she asked.

"Sure thing. Alex and I will be right out," Charlotte promised.

Ava couldn't escape fast enough. She hurried down the stairs, said hello to a woman wiping the counter in the kitchen, who she assumed was Carmen, and headed out into the late afternoon sunlight. She took big gulps of fresh air.

"Hey," Ava said, approaching Ben. He looked about nine years old. She nabbed the basketball as it ricocheted off the backboard yet again. "Can I play too?"

Ben shrugged. "Sure."

Ava aimed, then let the ball glide off her fingertips and swoosh through the hoop.

Ben watched in openmouthed amazement. Then he grinned, and they began to play. Ava liked how easy it was with guys. Especially if you could throw a ball.

She still couldn't figure out Charlotte. All afternoon, she'd been so nice. The way she'd been earlier in the week when Ava had first met her. Ava wanted to ask her why she was so rude to Emily and Lindsey, but so far the time hadn't seemed right. And maybe it didn't matter.

"You're good," Ben said as Ava sank another basket.

"My big brother taught me," she said. "Let me

give you some tips. Your weight is too far back in your heels. Try it like this."

Ben mimicked her stance. He sent the ball toward the hoop. It bounced off the rim.

"Closer!" Ava cried, going for the rebound. "Whoa!" She lost her balance and stumbled as a blur of curly black fur streaked across the lawn and into the shrubs bordering the yard.

"Harvey! Harvey!" Carmen stood by the back door, waving her arms. "He escaped again! Ben!"

Ben took off after the dog. Ava hesitated, then hurried after both of them.

Together they trampled through the bushes. Twigs scratched Ava's shins. She kept going. She spotted Harvey's black fur up ahead.

Suddenly Harvey made an abrupt turn, circling the edge of the property. Ava and Ben twisted back through the bushes. Carmen stayed on the stone patio, yelling for the dog. Harvey didn't seem to hear or care.

"Go right. We'll corner him!" Ben told Ava.

Ava broke right. She felt as if she were on the football field running a play. But a dog was much harder to catch than a football. She had no idea where this ball of fur was heading.

Harvey darted through the bushes once more

and into the neighbor's yard. Ava and Ben followed. Across another yard. Through another neighbor's vegetable garden. *Good-bye to that head of lettuce,* Ava thought as she trampled more veggies than she dodged.

Harvey ran faster.

Ava kept up the chase. Ben struggled to keep close. The dog was still in sight.

Closer . . . closer . . .

Up ahead, she spotted a low stone wall. A big house rose beyond it. The largest Texas flag she'd ever seen flew from a pole in the yard. Harvey slowed as he approached the wall.

Seizing the opportunity, Ava dove forward, arms outstretched, and grabbed Harvey's fur. She pulled Harvey toward her, grasping the small dog around its middle.

Touchdown! Ava thought.

She and Harvey lay on the ground, both panting, both exhausted.

"Harvey!" Ben cried. He slid beside Ava and scooped his dog into his arms.

Harvey licked Ben's nose.

"You have one crazy dog," Ava said.

"He's not crazy," Ben protested, hugging his dog fiercely. "Everything here scares him. The grass, the trees, the other animals. He's kind of like Charlotte."

Ava thought about this. Charlotte didn't seem scared at all. Charlotte had bulldozed forward and taken down the popular kids. And she hadn't even been in school a week!

"Do *you* like it here?" Ava asked.

Ben shrugged. "Don't know yet. It was kind of sudden. Mom told us on a Monday, and by Friday some moving company had packed us and we were on the plane."

"Really?" Ava's parents had discussed the pros and cons of their move with their kids for weeks before her dad accepted the coaching job.

"Mom's like that. She works for Rouge." Ben looked to Ava for a reaction, but she had none. "Okay . . . most girls scream when they hear that. It's a big makeup company."

"Never heard of it," Ava admitted. "But I'm not into makeup. My twin sister would probably be drooling."

"They chose Mom to head up the Southwest division, and they needed her right away, so— boom!—here we are," Ben explained. "My dad already had a business trip scheduled to Hong Kong, so he flew off and well, Charlotte and I were kind of dropped in Texas. It's been weird."

"That's rough," Ava said. Her parents never flew off on business trips.

"Who lives here?" Ben asked suddenly, staring up at the huge flag.

Ava looked at the big house. An ASHLAND TIGERS 1979 STATE CHAMPS banner was strung across the porch. A second banner, WHITTAKER #34, flew below it. "I'm guessing this is Floyd Whittaker's house. He's crazy about Ashland football. He runs the Booster Club."

"Hey, maybe Harvey ran here because he wants to join the football team!" Ben cried.

"He would be a good running back," Ava agreed. "Actually, so would you. You're fast."

"You think?" Ben grinned.

Ava nodded.

"Something smells good," he said.

Ava inhaled the spicy aroma of charcoal smoke. She glanced over the wall. Floyd Whittaker stood in the center of the largest concrete patio she'd ever seen. His back was to them, but Ava spotted a large stainless-steel barbecue grill.

"He must be making dinner," she said.

"I'd like some," Ben said. Harvey whimpered.

"So would old Harvey here. Maybe Harvey was coming for some barbecued ribs."

"He's a smart dog," Ava said. Then she heard Alex call her name. Ben carried Harvey, and they walked to the house. Their mom's SUV waited in the driveway.

"Took you long enough. I have your backpack." Alex opened the car's back door and tossed both packs in. Then she waved to Charlotte and slid in too.

"Alex told me about the Power," Charlotte said before Ava could follow.

"She did?" Ava shifted her weight. She didn't want to talk about this.

"I think it's amazing," Charlotte said. "I've never known anyone with psychic abilities."

"We don't—" Ava didn't get to finish.

"Ave, come on!" her mom called.

"Got to go," Ava said, and hurried into the car. "Thanks for having us!"

"Alex has a dentist appointment," Mrs. Sackett said, starting up the car. "Ava, I'll drop you at home with Tommy. I left sandwiches for dinner. And Luke is coming to tutor you tonight."

Ava nodded. Luke was in high school with Tommy. Ever since she'd found out she had

ADHD, he'd been helping her twice a week with her homework. Luke focused her, and he was fun to be around.

"What about Daddy?" Alex asked.

"He's still at the school. It'll be a late night with the coaches." Their mom gripped the steering wheel tightly. "I can't wait for this game to be over."

For a moment, they were all silent, thinking about tomorrow's big game. Then Ava told Mrs. Sackett about the dog chase.

"You're awfully quiet, Alex," their mom commented at the end of the story. "Nothing to add?"

Alex had never let Ava tell a full story without jumping in. Now Alex typed furiously on her phone.

"What's up?" Ava asked, whispering so their mom couldn't hear them.

"Everyone is talking about it." Alex showed her the screen.

"It?" Ava had a sinking feeling she knew what "it" was.

"Our Power. How we found Rosa's bracelet." Alex beamed.

"What?" Ava winced. She should have told Alex the truth about how she'd found the bracelet earlier. Now the whole school knew.

"Actually, they're kind of only talking about

me. They don't seem to think you were involved. I promise I'll set everyone straight." Alex turned back to her phone.

Ava grabbed her wrist. "Oh, no! Leave me out of this."

"Really?" Alex shrugged. "It's fun to have everyone be so amazed, don't you think?"

"Ava, scoot. Alex is going to be late." Mrs. Sackett had pulled into their driveway.

"Alex, about that . . ." Ava's voice trailed off.

"Finish that thought later," Mrs. Sackett commanded. "And tell Tommy to leave a sandwich for Alex. Out you go."

Ava had no choice. She got out and watched Alex drive away, believing they had the Power.

Ava scooped a stray football off their lawn. She twirled it in her hands, letting a new thought poke the corners of her mind. If she told her sister, Alex would probably say Rosa's bracelet didn't prove anything. Alex would still insist that they did have powers. They had worn the same outfit and bought Coach the same present.

What did it matter to her what Alex believed? Or what the kids at school believed?

She could just leave it alone and everyone would be happy.

CHAPTER NINE

Alex was pleased with her costume. It was pretty genius, if she said so herself.

And she had to say so, because no one was home to say it.

Ava had left the house early for Saturday football practice. The middle school team planned to walk together to the high school stadium to watch the game. Alex hoped Ava had remembered to pack a costume. She hadn't had a chance to remind her last night. Ava had showered after Luke left and fell asleep while Alex was downstairs watching an eighties rom-com with her mom.

Tommy and Coach had left this morning right after Ava. Why they needed hours in the locker room to get ready for the game was a mystery to Alex.

And Mrs. Sackett had just run to the store, because the bags of mini chocolate bars she'd hidden away for trick-or-treaters earlier in the month were now basically bags of empty wrappers. Alex shook her head. Her mom should have chosen a better hiding place. She knew that when Coach couldn't sleep, he headed right for the candy.

And before the big game this week, there had been a lot of sleepless nights.

Alex checked the clock. They were cutting it awfully close. Kickoff was in less than thirty minutes. Luckily, the coach's family had reserved seats.

Alex turned her attention back to the fork on the kitchen table. She visualized it rising up, up, up. She stared at it until her eyes crossed and she had to blink.

The fork lay there. Not moving. Not levitating.

"I need Ava," she said aloud.

"You need Ava for what?" The kitchen door banged open, and an orange-and-black tiger hurried in and tossed two bags of sour lollipops onto the counter. "The drugstore was totally wiped out. This is all they had left."

Alex decided not to answer the Ava question.

Right before the big game was not the time to tell her mom that they had psychic powers. She wasn't quite sure when the right time was.

"You look cute, but your costume isn't going to win for originality in this town," Alex told her mom. "I do like your whiskers, though."

"Grrrr," Mom growled, and her furry tiger ears tilted atop her head. "I have to support the team." She took a closer look at Alex. "Is that my glass bowl?"

Alex nodded. She'd turned it upside down and wrapped the open bottom with a red scarf. "It's not the good one. It's that gross one that the wilted flowers from Great-Aunt Leslie came in. It's going to be my crystal ball. Can you guess what I am?"

Alex had dressed in a long velvet skirt, a white ruffled blouse, and short black boots. She'd wrapped a purple scarf around her hair, which she'd worn extra curly. Several silk scarves hung down from her waist, and many gold and silver chains circled her neck.

"You're a fortune-teller!" Mrs. Sackett grinned. "I like it."

Alex liked it too. She liked it, because it felt real. She could find things and link thoughts with Ava, and that was amazing.

The stadium was packed when they arrived. Werewolves, vampires, bunnies, witches, and hundreds of tigers all stomped as the Ashland High marching band played the school song to announce the team.

"There he is!" Mrs. Sackett grasped Alex's hand as Coach jogged onto the field behind the last player. The stands erupted in cheers.

Coach looked serious, holding his clipboard. He glanced up at the forty yard line, where they had their reserved seats, and gave Mrs. Sackett a quick nod. Mrs. Sackett nodded back. They did this before every home game. Alex wasn't sure what it meant exactly, but she knew it was a good-luck thing. Coach was superstitious that way. He was wearing the socks he'd worn during the last game they won, sure that his smelly feet juices were lucky and would help them win again. He only washed them when they lost.

Alex cringed. Those socks must be vile by now. The Tigers had won a lot this season.

The game started. Tommy was only third-string quarterback, so he sat on the players' bench. Alex spotted Ava in the bleachers a few sections away, sitting with the middle school football team.

"What is she?" she asked her mom.

Mrs. Sackett studied Ava for a bit. "A pioneer, maybe?"

"Really? You think Ava went all *Little House on the Prairie*? That seems odd," Alex said, standing for a better look.

"I see a blue bonnet," Mrs. Sackett said. "And a green shirt and green shorts."

"I'm completely clueless," Alex admitted. She texted Ava. Then she laughed. "Classic! She's the state flower of Texas. She's a bluebonnet. Get it?"

Her mom chuckled. "How did she even know what the flower is?"

"We learn lots of Texas facts in school," Alex said. "It's kind of cool, because I never knew that stuff about Massachusetts."

When the dance team came out for the halftime show, their neighbors, Dr. and Mr. Cahill, showed up to sit with Mrs. Sackett, and Alex went off to join Ava and her friends.

She squeezed in next to Lindsey. "This is not

my party costume," Lindsey informed her. She wore a red lifeguard shirt, white makeup on her nose, sunglasses on her head, and a whistle around her neck. "I'm going all out tonight."

Alex peered into her crystal ball. "I am the Great Alexandra, and I can see into the future. I see that your party is going to be epic."

"You are very wise, O Great Alexandra!" Lindsey grinned.

Corey leaned over. He had green makeup smeared over his face and what she guessed were aluminum-foil antennae attached to his baseball cap. But he still looked cute. "What do you see for the Ashland Tigers?" he asked.

"Victory, of course!" Alex said.

"Well, they better get to it," Corey remarked. The first half had ended with a score of 0–0.

"PJ's doing okay, right?" Alex called to Ava, who was sitting a few people down. PJ Kelly played quarterback. Alex didn't think it was PJ's fault that the game was scoreless. He'd been throwing well and trying to run down the field. He just kept getting tackled.

"He's doing fine," Ava called back.

"Rutland's defense is awesome," Corey put in. "They're not letting us complete our passes."

"Our defense is holding strong too," Owen added. "They can't score off us either."

"Coach must be going nuts in the locker room right now," Ava said, "trying to motivate our guys to score."

"We're not losing," Alex reminded her.

"But we're not winning," Ava said.

They shared a knowing look. They hadn't started preparing for Coach's birthday brunch. They hadn't even talked about it. Alex felt it would jinx the game. She thought Ava felt the same.

It's our telepathic thing again, Alex realized. She flashed Ava a secretive smile.

By the end of the final quarter, the game was tied 14–14. Alex watched the scoreboard clock tick down. In a minute, they'd go into overtime. She watched her dad pace the sidelines. His arms were folded, his eyebrows knitted together, his mouth set in a grim line. Alex chewed her bottom lip in frustration. She wished she could do something to make the players on the field score.

But all she could do was cheer. She felt useless. And questions kept swirling in her head.

Would they have to leave, if the team didn't make it to the next round in the play-offs? She was pretty sure the school liked her dad and wouldn't fire him. But what did she know? Ashland was crazy when it came to football. If they had to leave, would they move back to Massachusetts? Would her friends there welcome her? Did she even want to go back?

Alex glanced at her Ashland friends, all crowded together. She liked them. She liked it here. A lot. The fans around her let out a collective groan as some huge player tackled PJ before he could complete his pass. Alex couldn't bear to keep watching.

"Did Charlotte ever come to the game?" Alex called to Ava to get her mind off the field.

Ava shook her head. "I didn't see her."

"That girl is totally rude," Lindsey remarked. Emily and Rosa, who sat behind them, nodded vigorously.

Emily leaned forward. "She mocked me for saying 'y'all' yesterday when I came up to her in the hall."

"She hates us," Rosa added. "I don't know why."

"She hates Texas," Kylie offered.

"She better not mess with Texas or else," Corey declared, puffing out his chest.

"Or else what?" Owen challenged.

Corey grinned. "Or else I'll lasso her in my pickup truck!"

Lindsey elbowed him. "You don't have a pickup truck. Your parents drive SUVs."

Corey smiled. "It was a Texas joke."

"Hey, I have a pickup truck and a lasso," Kylie announced proudly. "No joke!"

"Charlotte's really not mean," Alex said. She liked Charlotte. She felt bad that her new friend wasn't here to defend herself. "You should give her another chance. Right, Ava?"

"Right," Ava agreed. Then she screamed. "Guys! Look! Look!"

Alex stood on her tiptoes to see over the tall guy in front of her. PJ dodged to the left and then the right. He pulled his arm back and fired the ball downfield. The stadium grew quiet, tracking the arc of the ball. It landed in the outstretched arms of Tyler Whitely, and the Ashland fans roared. The Tigers' blockers expertly cleared the way, and Tyler ran down the field. The stadium bleachers shook and rattled with cheers and stamping feet.

"He's doing it!" Corey cried.

"Go, go!" Alex screamed.

Coach Sackett moved his arms like a windmill, as if that could propel his player farther down the field. Tyler dove for the end zone. The referee raised his arms.

"He did it!" Lindsey shrieked.

"The big win!" Ava yelled.

"We won!" Alex cried. The band erupted in a victory song. The cheerleaders flipped on the sideline. And Coach Sackett smiled for the first time that week.

"We are the Ashland Tigers, hear us roar!" Alex sang along with her friends as they filed out of the stadium.

"Alex! Ava! Alex!"

A voice rang out over the noise. Alex looked around, uncertain where it came from and who was calling her. The parking lot was filled with people in costume. Little kids lined up for Trunk-or-Treat, where they collected candy from different decorated cars. Kylie was helping Owen at his family's car.

"Alex! Ava!" Charlotte pushed her way forward. Her eyes were puffy and her voice hoarse. She wasn't in a costume, and her knees and palms were streaked with dirt.

"What's wrong?" Alex cried.

"Harvey." Charlotte leaned forward, gasping for breath. "I was home alone, and Harvey ran away. It was my fault. I left the back door open. I've looked everywhere. I can't find him."

"We can help look," Ava offered.

Charlotte shook her head. "I need more than that. It's an emergency. Ben went out with my mom. Harvey is his best friend. I can't tell him I lost his best friend!" She sounded hysterical.

"What do you need?" Alex asked.

"You! Your Power! I need you to find Harvey with your Power!" Charlotte cried, grabbing onto one of Alex's many scarves.

"But—I don't know—it's a dog—I'm not sure—" Alex fumbled for an answer. She hadn't had a chance to ask Ava how the whole bracelet vision had come to her. She needed more time to understand the Power and how it worked.

"You've done it before." Emily placed her hand on Alex's shoulder. "You can find her dog."

"Alex can totally do this," Rosa agreed.

A warmth spread through Alex. Her friends believed in her.

"Hold up." Ava stepped forward. "Charlotte, this is Harvey we're talking about. Not a bracelet. We need to move fast."

"Our telepathy thing does take time. . . ." Alex's voice trailed off.

"There are a lot of cars pulling away from the parking lot now," Kylie pointed out.

Charlotte's skin turned the same green as Corey's alien makeup. "Oh no! Harvey can't get hit by a car!"

"That's why we need to search your neighborhood now. There are a lot of us. We can go in groups." Ava gestured to all their friends.

Charlotte's eyes darted around, taking in the large group for the first time. "No! Not them! I just need you two!" she cried.

"Well, gee, thanks," Lindsey quipped.

"We should *all* go," Ava insisted.

"I'm not going," Lindsey said. "I'm getting ready for my party. Rosa, Emily, come on."

"But, Lindz, I want to see Alex find the dog," Emily said.

"Me too." Rosa pulled out her phone. "We can film it and upload to Madame Sibyl's site. Alex will be famous."

"Ooh! Maybe Sibyl will ask Alex to be on her TV show," Emily gushed. She pulled Alex close. "We would look so good on TV."

"Who said you would go on TV too?" Rosa asked.

"I introduced Alex to Sibyl. I'm responsible for her accessing her undiscovered power," Emily said.

"Miss New York City doesn't want us." Lindsey

glared at Charlotte. "She made that clear. She thinks she's too good for us."

"No, no. That's not it." Charlotte was frantic now.

"Could have fooled me," Lindsey muttered. Corey nodded.

Alex's head throbbed. Her friends were fighting and she didn't understand why. Charlotte's dog was missing. She needed to use her mind to find him, not to puzzle out why Charlotte didn't like Lindsey, Emily, and Rosa.

"Charlotte, they just want to help," Alex said in a quiet voice.

"I don't need them. Just you two." Tears welled in Charlotte's eyes.

"What did we ever do to you?" Lindsey planted her hands on her hips.

Charlotte stared down at her flip-flops. Her whole body trembled. "I want to go home."

"So go," said Lindsey.

"Yeah, we were only trying to find your dog." Emily stood shoulder to shoulder with Lindsey.

"I don't think she means her house here," Ava piped up.

"That doesn't give her the right to be so rude," Lindsey pointed out.

"Fine! I'm sorry!" Charlotte threw up her

hands. "Everyone can come. I need help."

For a moment, no one spoke.

"I'll help," Xander offered.

"Me too," said Corey.

"We're only coming because we want to see Alex and Ava do their special thing," Emily said finally. Rosa nodded.

"We don't do anything special," Ava protested.

"Yes, we do," Alex interjected.

"Al—" Ava began again.

"We can try, Ave. Right? Can't we? Just try, I mean?" Alex sent her sister a pleading look.

"Let's just go!" Charlotte cried impatiently.

"Come on. The Power of Two. That's what Madame Sibyl said," Emily prodded. "Psychic twins go! Go!"

Corey and Xander took up the cheer. "Psychic twins, go!"

Alex felt Charlotte grab her hand. She barely had time to hand Mrs. Sackett's glass bowl to Ava before they were running down the school's driveway toward Charlotte's house. Her fortune-teller scarves flew around her. Ava, Emily, Rosa, Corey, Xander, and even Lindsey followed.

Can we do this? Alex wondered. *Yes, we can,* she decided. *I think we really can!*

CHAPTER TEN

I never should have let Alex say yes, Ava realized. She ripped off her bonnet, cradled her mom's glass bowl, and raced after her sister. What was going on? Halloween was supposed to be spooky, not crazy!

Ava craned her neck, searching for a fluffy black dog. If she could just find Harvey, then Alex wouldn't have to try whatever it was she was going to try. She felt guilty. If she'd only told Alex about the bracelet, her sister might not have been so quick to say yes.

Or maybe she would have. Ava never knew with Alex. Alex liked to help others. She also liked to be the center of attention. And she definitely seemed to believe they had telepathic powers. Did she know something that Ava didn't?

She followed the others into Charlotte's backyard.

"Ava!" Alex waved her over. The group had gathered on the patio.

Ava eyed Ben's basketball, abandoned on the court. She'd so love to shoot some hoops right now. Instead she spun in a slow circle, surveying the Huangs' large yard. "Harvey! Hey, Harvey! Here, boy!" Ava yelled.

"What are you doing?" Corey asked.

"It seems like the logical way to start." Ava almost laughed. How ironic! Now she was the logical twin!

"I've called him a zillion times. Try using your psychic powers," Charlotte begged Alex as Ava continued to call for Harvey. "Please."

"I need Ava to help me," Alex said.

"Do you have Harvey's leash? Or a favorite toy?" Emily asked Charlotte.

"Why?" Ava asked.

"So you and Alex can pick up Harvey's vibe. Kind of like how the police have search dogs sniff a missing person's clothes," Emily explained. "It will help you locate him."

"The Sackett twins are now the search dogs searching for a dog!" Xander hooted.

"Not funny!" Ava gave him a light punch on the arm.

Charlotte ran inside and quickly returned with a blue braided leash. She placed it in Alex's outstretched hands.

"I'm ready." Rosa positioned her phone to videotape.

"Ava?" Alex didn't have to ask. Ava knew the question. She couldn't say no. Not now. Not in front of everyone.

"Fine. We'll try," Ava agreed. She turned to Rosa. "But no filming. I'm serious."

Alex nodded. "Ava and I have to be alone. Someplace quiet so we can focus."

"We'll go by the swing set," Ava said. "You guys should look for Harvey. Yell for him. Search the neighborhood."

Corey gave her a fake salute and headed off with Xander in one direction. Charlotte ran off alone in the other.

Ava scrambled up the ladder that led into an enclosed area at the top of the slide. When her head bumped the log-cabin-like roof, she sat. Alex followed, her long skirt tangling around her feet.

Ava stared out the cutout opening for the slide. "What now?"

"We hold Harvey's leash and hold hands and try to see where he is," Alex said matter-of-factly. "Visualize him."

Ava intertwined her fingers with Alex's.

Alex began to hum. A low sound, as if she were really concentrating.

Ava thought about Harvey. *Harvey. Harvey.* Where was he? The last time she was here, he'd sprinted to the Whittakers' big house. Wait! Someone should check there.

"Hold up." She dropped Alex's hand and her end of the leash. She peered down the slide. Rosa and Emily waited below. Lindsey lounged on a cushioned chair on the patio, playing on her phone with a scowl on her face. "Someone needs to go to the Whittakers'," she called down to the other girls. "They're a couple of houses away. Harvey ran off there the other day. Maybe he went back."

"I'll do it," Rosa offered. "I know them." She took off with Emily, and Ava returned to Alex.

"We need to really focus," Alex reminded her. "You need to be totally in tune with me. And Harvey."

"I am." Ava held on to her sister's hand and the leash.

Five minutes, she decided. *If Alex doesn't get some sort of vision-thing in five minutes, I'll tell her that the Power doesn't work. That it never worked.*

Ava thought about Harvey. All at once, her stomach growled. Now all she could think about was food. She hadn't eaten since the banana this morning before practice. She wished she'd bought a hamburger at the game. The stadium snack bar had surprisingly good burgers. And there were sweet pickles at the condiment bar you could put on them.

Stop it! she scolded herself. *Think about poor Harvey.*

And then she recalled the smell of barbecue when they'd chased Harvey to the Whittakers'. Yum! She'd love some barbecue now.

Hey! Maybe Harvey went back there today to find more barbecue. Maybe the dog was hungry. Maybe he liked Texas barbecue.

"No dog in the Whittakers' yard!" Rosa's voice called up to them a few minutes later.

Ava groaned. She'd been sure they'd find Harvey there.

"Al?" she whispered.

Alex opened her eyes. "Did you see him? Did you get a vision?"

"No." Ava felt horrible. Alex sounded so hopeful. "There's something I need to tell you."

"What?"

And then Ava remembered. Not far down the street from Charlotte's gated community was Fighting Tiger BBQ, the main competitor of Jimmy's Pit Bar-B-Q, where her family often ate. If Harvey really did like barbecue, it'd make sense for him to run to Fighting Tiger. Everyone raved about their baby back ribs and oak-smoked brisket.

"I have an idea! Come with me!" Ava slid down the slide. Alex slid after her.

"Did you do it? Did it work?" Emily asked.

"Do you know where the dog is?" Rosa cried.

"We'll be right back!" Ava called. "Stay here." She grabbed Alex's hand and pulled her toward the road.

"Do you know? Do you?" Alex cried. She ran alongside Ava. Her long, colorful scarves rippled behind her like the tail of a kite.

"Maybe. I hope so," Ava said. "Hurry!"

"I'm trying!" Alex called, as she tripped on a scarf and nearly face-planted.

"These have to go." Ava grabbed the scarves and gave a yank, and they both heard a loud *rrrrrip*.

"You tore my skirt!" Alex cried.

"Sorry," Ava apologized. "Your costume was slowing us down."

"I can't believe you! What am I going to wear to Lindsey's party?" Alex demanded.

"We'll figure it out later. It's not like you were going to wear the same costume twice today," Ava pointed out.

"You didn't know that," Alex said, inspecting the tear.

"I did. I know *you*, remember?" Ava said. "Come on. Let's find Harvey." She began to sprint again. Alex followed, running a lot faster now.

"This place?" Alex asked, as Ava stopped in front of Fighting Tiger BBQ. "Did you visualize a tiger?"

"Not exactly." Ava looked around. The parking lot was packed with fans from the game. The smell of tangy barbecue sauce wafted out of the restaurant and made her stomach grumble again. Going inside would be dangerous.

"You go ask about Harvey inside. I'll check the parking lot," Ava told Alex.

"But you haven't told me why we're here," Alex protested. "How did you do it?"

"Later," Ava promised. "Harvey! Harvey!" she called as she searched by each and every car.

Alex met her in the lot behind the building. "No one inside has seen him."

"He's not in the parking lot either." Ava sighed. Her idea hadn't been right, after all. "I'm sorry."

"Why are you sorry?" Alex asked.

Ava couldn't keep it from her sister any longer. She told Alex about how she'd really found Rosa's bracelet. And why she'd brought them to the barbecue place.

Alex was quiet for a long time.

"Aren't you going to yell at me?" When Alex was quiet, it made Ava nervous. She always had something to say.

Alex shook her head. "You don't think it's a little bit possible that we have powers?"

"Were you able to see the bracelet or see Harvey?" Ava asked.

"No, but that doesn't mean we aren't telepathic," Alex protested. "I feel it. I do."

"I guess." Ava noticed a stone path behind the restaurant. They walked along it. Park benches lined the path. The path led to a large concrete plaza with a covered bandstand at one end.

"What's this place?" Ava asked.

"Maybe they have concerts here?" Alex guessed. "What am I going to tell Emily? And Charlotte? I let them call us psychic. They're going to think I made it all up."

Ava didn't answer. A shadow had caught her attention.

She inched her way along the side of the bandstand. Slowly, quietly. She crouched down, extended her palms, and called softly. "Here, boy!"

In an instant Harvey was sniffing her hands. Ava petted his curly black fur.

"He *was* looking for barbecue! You're a great detective, Ava!" Alex cried.

Ava grinned. "I don't think he was looking for barbecue. I think he was looking for concrete."

"Concrete?" Alex repeated.

Ava pointed to a puddle on the ground. "I think this feels more like home. Harvey's not used to grass."

"Gross!" Alex cried.

"Let's get you to Charlotte and Ben," Ava said, grabbing Harvey's collar.

"Hey! Hey!" An older man in a sauce-stained

white apron waved to them as they walked back through the parking lot. "Good! I see you found your dog. Are you two the Sackett twins?"

Ava nodded uncertainly. How did he know them?

"I'm Jay Grasing, owner of this place here." He beamed at them, his gray-blue eyes bright. "Please tell your dad that that was one amazing game today. I played for the Tigers back in the day. His use of the defense was inspired. You girls must be very happy with the big win."

"Very happy," Ava agreed. It was still so weird when strangers recognized them just because of their dad.

"Wait right there. I'm going to bring you a big bag of barbecue. On the house." He reached out and patted Harvey's head. "And a bit of brisket for your pooch, too."

"Hear that, Harvey? You're going to get some barbecue, after all," Ava said.

"So what are you going to tell them?" Alex asked Ava as they walked toward Charlotte's house.

"About finding Harvey? I'll tell them whatever

you want me to tell them," Ava offered.

"I don't want to lie," Alex said.

"Then don't." Ava held the foil-lined bag of meat in one hand. In the other hand, she grasped a long piece of twine Jay Grasing had fashioned into a leash for Harvey.

"But I like how everyone thinks we're so special," Alex said.

"Lots of people in Ashland seem to think we're pretty special, and they don't even know what the Power is," Ava pointed out. "Look, we got free food."

"That's different," Alex scoffed, as they rounded Charlotte's wide lawn.

Alex couldn't put words to her disappointment. She had truly thought she and Ava had a connection, more than just being twins. She wasn't ready to give up on it, even though it hadn't been any psychic power that helped them find the missing bracelet or the missing dog.

"Harvey!" Charlotte shrieked. She flung her arms around her dog. Everyone crowded around. Rosa, despite her earlier promise, filmed the homecoming on her phone.

"You did it. You really did it!" Emily exclaimed over and over. She raised Alex's arm triumphantly.

All her friends gave her admiring and incredulous looks.

Except Ava. Ava raised her eyebrows, questioning Alex.

Alex knew her sister wouldn't rat her out. But she also knew that Ava trusted her to fess up.

She wanted to tell them. But the words caught in her dry throat.

"You two are the absolute best!" Charlotte wrapped one arm around each twin's shoulder.

Lindsey shook her head in disgust.

"Wait." Charlotte stepped over to her. "I'm not done. You are *all* the best." She spread her arms to indicate everyone. "You all helped me look for Harvey. I didn't deserve your help. I've been acting horribly."

Lindsey narrowed her eyes. "Why?"

"Why was I acting like that?" Charlotte twisted her fingers. She seemed unable to explain.

"I think I know," Ava said. "The move to Texas was shoved on you. You were angry, and you didn't want to be here."

Charlotte nodded. "You have no idea."

"But I do. Kind of," Ava said. "When I moved here, it was strange and scary. Any new place is. But now I like it. I feel like a true Texas kid."

"Really?" Charlotte seemed surprised. "I wanted you, Alex, and me to be friends, because all three of us were from the East Coast. We'd stick together. Just us." Charlotte's voice grew quiet. "If I only hung out with you two, I could forget I was in Texas."

"I don't get it. What's wrong with Texas?" Corey demanded.

"Nothing," Alex said. She now understood. "Charlotte decided to hate Texas and everyone in it, because if she made Texas friends, then she couldn't be angry at her family for the move."

"That's exactly it," Charlotte said. "But I was wrong. You guys are really nice. I'm sorry."

"So no more cheerleader jokes?" Lindsey asked.

Charlotte grinned. "How about no more barbecue jokes?"

"I actually like those jokes. I'm not a big barbecue fan," Lindsey admitted. "My sister is making mozzarella sticks for my party. I'm thinking about giving up meat altogether."

"Traitor!" Corey joked, reaching into Ava's bag of barbecue.

"I love mozzarella sticks." Charlotte looked at Lindsey. "Can I still come to your party?"

"Definitely," said Lindsey. "Do you have a costume?"

"Not yet," said Charlotte.

"Me either," Ava admitted. "My bluebonnet idea was lame."

Alex inspected her torn skirt. "I don't have a costume either."

"Well, you girls better get thinking! My party is in a couple of hours," Lindsey said. Then she eyed Alex. "Oh, I just thought of the best surprise for the party. It will blow everyone away!"

"What is it?" Alex hated surprises.

"You'll have to wait and see," Lindsey sang, heading off with Rosa. "I need to go get the decorations up."

"I bet Alex knows what your surprise is right now," Emily said, following them. "Alex can see into the future."

Alex stayed quiet. She still couldn't bring herself to say, "No, I can't."

CHAPTER ELEVEN

Alex let out a high-pitched shriek. A bat swooped low, brushing her ear in the darkness. She flailed her arms and swatted desperately at it.

"Relax. It's fake!" Ava laughed. Then she showed her sister the rubber bat swinging from clear fishing line on the lamppost. "Boo!"

"It's creepy out here," Alex said, her heart still thumping. Halloween always made her jumpy.

"Creepy fun," Charlotte said. "Ashland really takes its Halloween decorations seriously."

The path to Lindsey's house glowed with grinning jack-o'-lanterns. Cobwebs draped the front porch, and a life-size skeleton guarded the door. Spooky music floated from the windows into the moonless night.

"See?" Ava grinned. "Texas scores another point."

"I guess it does." Charlotte grinned back.

"Ready?" Alex said. "We need to walk in together."

Ava and Charlotte nodded.

"Okay, let's do this." Alex rang the doorbell.

Cinderella, a pirate, and a zombie answered. Alex immediately recognized Lindsey, Owen, and Kylie.

"Yee-ha!" Lindsey cried. "Howdy, pardners! You three look amazing!"

"We wanted to show our Texas spirit," Charlotte said.

Alex, Ava, and Charlotte modeled their cowgirl costumes—fringed shirts and vests, denim skirts, cowboy hats, and cowboy boots. They'd borrowed the boots from Kylie.

"Pure rodeo." Kylie nodded her approval.

"Alex and I are Texans now, through and through," Ava said. "Even without the costumes."

"And proud of it," Alex added with a whoop.

"I'm working on it," Charlotte admitted.

Lindsey pulled them into the party. Kids in costume milled about everywhere. A long table displayed her sister's amazing food—pumpkin cupcakes, witch's brew, bat wings, skeleton fingers, eyeball salad, and werewolf dip. Alex bit into a skeleton finger. Warm cheese oozed out. Yum! Sloane's mozzarella sticks.

"High five!" a boy in army fatigues said. He raised his hand for Alex to slap.

"Uh, sure." She lifted her hand, although she only slightly recognized him from math class. "Why?"

"We're on to the next round of the play-offs. Then Ashland is going to state. We are on our way. I can feel it. Can you?" he cried.

"Totally," Alex agreed.

"Our team too," Corey added, coming up behind her. "The middle school team is also advancing."

"Time to celebrate!" Lindsey called out. Then she turned up the music.

Alex walked through the party, admiring costumes, talking to kids, and eating Sloane's scrumptious pumpkin cupcakes. She was having a great time, especially when she and Ella from her debate club teamed up to win the toilet-paper mummy-wrap contest.

Then Lindsey tapped her shoulder.

"You know, right?"

"Know what?" Alex straightened her white cowboy hat. The mummy wrap had left her costume askew.

"My surprise. Emily said you'd know without me telling you. Do you like it?" Lindsey asked eagerly.

Alex didn't know what Lindsey's surprise was. She had no idea at all. Did that mean that Ava was right? That she truly wasn't psychic? Alex's stomach twisted, and not from the cupcakes.

"Didn't I have the best idea?" Lindsey asked when Alex didn't answer.

"Great idea." Alex forced out the words. She was sure Lindsey had come up with something fabulous. *This isn't a lie,* she told herself.

So why did she feel so horrible?

"Ava, there you are!" Lindsey waved Ava over. Charlotte followed. "Everyone is waiting for you two. There's even a line. Can you believe it?"

"What's she talking about?" Ava whispered to Alex.

Alex shrugged. She followed Lindsey down a hallway toward the back of the house. All the lights were dimmed. Cobwebs covered the fixtures. A group of kids gathered at the doorway of what Alex assumed was a guest bedroom. Her eyes only momentarily landed on the flowered bedspread before her focus was drawn to a crudely constructed booth. A doorway covered by a sheet featured a handmade sign: TWIN FORTUNE-TELLERS SEE YOUR FUTURE!

Alex blinked. She blinked again. Lindsey couldn't be serious.

"Is this for *us*?" Ava voiced the question Alex was afraid to ask.

"It's perfect for Halloween," Lindsey gushed. "Spooky and paranormal."

"I'm going first!" Emily clawed her way to the front of the group. She wore a black cat suit and pointed cat ears.

"Then me," cried some kid in a witch's hat.

Alex stared at the fortune-teller's booth and all the kids eagerly waiting. And she knew. She finally knew, as clear as anything. *I can't do this,* she thought. *I can't tell these kids anything about their future. I can't find their missing hamster or misplaced cell phone.*

As much as she wanted to have the Power, she didn't. She didn't even know if the Power was a real thing. How had she gotten so caught up? Why had she let this go on for so long?

"No," she said finally.

"No? You don't want to read Emily's fortune first?" Lindsey asked.

"No, I can't do this." Alex looked to Ava. Ava nodded her encouragement. "*We* can't do this," Alex corrected.

"I know I didn't tell you before. I guess I should have asked—" Lindsey began.

"That's not it." Alex cut her off. She needed to tell the truth before she chickened out. Everyone listened expectantly. Once again she was in the spotlight. Just not the way she'd wanted. "We can't read fortunes. We can't see the future. I thought we could for a while, but I was fooling myself."

"What about my bracelet?" Rosa stepped forward.

"And Harvey?" Charlotte added.

"It wasn't the Power. It was Ava." Alex finally told them about Ava's detective work.

Alex readied herself for Emily, Rosa, and Lindsey to hate her. For all the kids to hate her. She'd lied to them. She'd lied to herself, but that didn't matter now.

"The Power thing was a great joke! I love it!" Charlotte cried out. "I mean, come on, you guys can't tell me you believed these Sackett girls are truly psychic?" she challenged the group of kids.

"I was onto them the whole time!" Corey laughed. "If Ava were psychic, she'd know where I was planning to throw the ball and be waiting downfield."

"Hey! I can catch any football you throw!" Ava retorted.

"But do you know what I'm thinking now?" Corey asked.

"No idea. But that's because you rarely do," Ava teased, lightening the mood. Several kids cheered. Alex was grateful to her. No one had laughed. Everyone acted as if they'd never thought she was psychic. As if they'd never believed she'd found things with her mind.

"But—but . . . my booth," Lindsey sputtered.

"No worries." Charlotte grabbed a black marker from a side table, dragged over a chair and stood on it, and began to write on the sign.

"Ta-da!" Charlotte stepped back and spotted a boy in a black gangster-style fedora. "May I?" she asked, replacing her cowboy hat with his hat. She tilted the brim and slipped the chair behind the sheet. With a flourish she pulled it back, sat on the chair, and announced, "I am open for business!"

Alex giggled when she read the new sign: NYC GIRL TELLS YOUR FASHION FUTURE.

"I will predict fashion for everyone. Guys and girls," Charlotte announced. "I'm wicked good at fashion."

"I do like your style," Rosa said, stepping forward. "What do you predict for me?" She entered the booth, and others crowded around.

Charlotte regarded Rosa. "Your arms are really toned from cheerleading. I see you rocking sleeveless tops more often. And red would be a good color with your skin tone."

"I have a red tank somewhere in my closet. It has silver studs around the collar." Rosa sounded uncertain.

"That's perfect! Embellished tanks are so fashion forward," Charlotte replied with a smile.

"I'll go find it. Thanks!" Rosa said.

"Me next!" Annelise cried.

"How awesome is she?" Ava whispered. "Charlotte totally came to our rescue."

"She's great," Alex agreed. She sensed Charlotte would become a good friend.

Emily moved alongside Alex. "I wanted you to have the Power. It really seemed like you did."

"I thought I did too. But I was wrong," Alex admitted.

"Maybe if we look at Sibyl's book again," Emily offered, not giving up. "Maybe if you practice more. I can help, if you want."

Alex shook her head. "I'm sorry, Em. I'm done with the Power. It doesn't work."

"You don't know that!" Emily protested. "If you only—"

"It doesn't work for me and Ava, that's what I'm saying," Alex said. "And I'm fine with that."

Ava wasn't sure how to act. Every time she said something, Tommy shot her a warning look. As if he were scared she'd say something to embarrass him, which was a distinct possibility. But sitting next to Alex in the backseat as they drove home from the party and not saying anything was just plain weird.

Finally Cassie swiveled in the passenger seat to talk to them. "I like your matching outfits."

"We don't normally do the twin matching thing, just so you know." If Tommy's girlfriend was going to be hanging out with them now,

Ava wanted to make that perfectly clear from the get-go.

"Oh, I got that." Cassie grinned. She was dressed as a jockey with riding pants, a red-and-white-checked silk shirt, and a riding helmet.

"There were three of us tonight. The three cowgirls. The three amigos," Alex said.

"And we won a contest," Ava offered, leaning her face between Tommy and Cassie. "Best Texan Costume! We let Charlotte take home the prize—a cupcake with a mini Texas flag on top."

"Your party sounds like fun," Cassie said.

"Where did you guys go tonight?" Ava asked.

"None of your business," Tommy said, turning onto their street.

"Tommy!" Cassie protested. "Be nicer to your sister."

Ava stuck her tongue out at him. She was going to like having Cassie around. "She's right . . . oh, wow!"

Tommy had pulled into the driveway, and Ava and Alex stared openmouthed at their front lawn.

"Did you know about this?" Alex asked, rolling down the window for a better look.

Tommy gave a mischievous grin. "My lips are sealed."

"It was the football team, wasn't it?" Ava squealed. "Wow! They covered every inch."

Every tree and bush was draped with toilet paper. Their mailbox and lamppost were wrapped so tightly, they appeared mummified. Strips hung from the gutters and fluttered like streamers in the slight breeze.

"Coach is going to go ballistic," Ava said. Coach loved football and cooking, but he also loved his lawn. He was always seeding and trimming.

Alex pointed to the light still on in their parents' bedroom window. "I bet he hasn't seen it yet."

And that was when Ava thought of it. The most perfect idea. "No one tell him tonight, okay?" she said.

"Why not?" Alex asked.

Ava told them all her brilliant plan.

CHAPTER TWELVE

"Surprise!" Ava cried the next morning. She jumped on her parents' bed to wake them.

"Happy birthday!" Alex called, flicking on the lights.

"Party time! Whoo! Whoo!" Tommy added, clapping his hands loudly.

Coach rubbed his eyes. His hair stuck up on one side. "What's all this?"

"Your Birthday Breakfast Bash," Ava announced. "Time to get up."

They pulled Coach from his bed. "Laura, did you put them up to this?" he asked.

"Not at all," Mrs. Sackett insisted with a bemused smile. She slipped on her robe. "I know nothing."

"Take this." Ava handed Coach the end of a long strand of toilet paper.

"And follow it," Alex said.

"I'm following toilet paper?" he asked incredulously.

"Exactly," said Tommy.

"Okay." He grinned at them, his green eyes twinkling. Ava could see he was clearly pleased with his birthday surprise. And with the big win.

The paper trail led out the bedroom door and downstairs to the front door.

"Now what?" he asked.

"Open the door!" they all cried.

He pushed it open and peered into the hazy morning light. For a moment he stood frozen, taking in the amazing sight.

They had kept last night's toilet paper exactly as it was, and Tommy had strung up their little white Christmas lights. Alex and Ava had added a big birthday banner and lots of colorful balloons.

Coach began to laugh. "Incredible! You three are incredible!"

"Not only us," Ava said. "The football team had a big part in the decorations."

"Time to eat," Alex said. She led their parents

to a folding table set up in the middle of the decorated yard. The table sported a bright-orange tablecloth and blue napkins—the Tigers' colors.

"Out here? In my pajamas?" Coach seemed horrified.

"Watch this. Instant privacy." Ava pulled closed a curtain made from two huge bedsheets that she'd strung between trees. The sheets blocked the view of the table from the street. She'd gotten the idea from Lindsey's fortune-telling booth.

"Football-shaped pancakes!" Coach cried with delight, as he surveyed all the food on the table.

"And gifts!" Ava gave him her football-shaped spatula. Alex gave him a platter that looked like a football field. She'd gone back to the store in the mall on Thursday and exchanged her spatula. Now their presents went together perfectly.

"One more game, and then we go to state!" Tommy reminded them, reaching for a large helping of bacon. They hadn't tried making chocolate-covered bacon. Just getting breakfast cooked and on the table had been challenging enough for the three of them. Adding boiling chocolate to the mix would have been asking for trouble.

"State is in Austin," Mrs. Sackett said. "I've

always wanted to visit. I hear they have great contemporary art galleries."

"And great live music," Tommy said.

"And great boutiques," Alex put in.

"If the team makes it, can we all go?" Ava asked Coach. "Please?"

"Absolutely," he said. "I'll need my whole family with me. We'll stay in a nice hotel."

I hope they spring for two rooms, Ava thought. In the past, they'd always crammed into one room. Mrs. Sackett and Coach in one bed, she and Alex sharing the other, and Tommy on a cot. *I don't want to share a bed with Alex,* she thought. *She snores.*

"I don't want to share with you, either, Ava," Alex retorted. "You kick at night."

"What are you talking about?" Tommy asked. "Ava didn't say anything."

Ava felt a shiver run down her spine. She locked eyes with Alex. *What had just happened between them?*

Ready for more
ALEX AND AVA?

Here's a sneak peek at the
next book in the **It Takes Two** series:

A Lot
to Tackle

"State! State! State!" The chant filled the crowded restaurant, echoing off the wood-beamed ceilings. Fans pounded the rhythm onto the worn tables. People just walking in immediately started stamping their feet to the beat in the aisles, dodging the waitresses balancing trays of steaming ribs and steaks.

Ava Sackett chanted so loudly that her throat hurt. The Ashland Tigers football team was going to the state championships!

She felt dizzy with excitement. Everyone in town was celebrating tonight, but Ava was sure that she was the happiest of all. This past summer, her family had moved from Massachusetts to Ashland, Texas, just so her dad could coach the high school team to victory. A lot of people had doubted him—but not Ava. She'd known Coach would lead the team all the way to the playoffs. And she knew he would win State, too.

Ava watched her twin sister Alex weave her way back from the bathroom at Fighting Tiger BBQ through the mass of fans. Strangers called out their congratulations. Alex beamed as she slid onto the bench next to Ava.

"Perfume much?" Ava teased, holding her nose. As usual, her twin sister had overly-spritzed herself with the honeysuckle body mist that she carried in her navy cross-body bag.

"You should try it," Alex teased back, knowing that unlike her, Ava refused to wear makeup and perfume. "Besides, I can't handle smelling like cooked cow."

"You don't have to put it that way!" Ava cried. Alex had become a vegetarian this year, so she wasn't a huge fan of the many barbeque restaurants in Texas.

Their older brother Tommy pushed in alongside Alex, squishing the twins closer together. Tommy had bulked up since he'd started playing high school football. The three of them barely fit onto the booth's bench.

The restaurant grew louder than other Friday

night post-game celebrations. People roared, pretending to be actual tigers. Ava inhaled. Alex's familiar sweet floral scent comforted her in the chaos. She wasn't big on crowds.

"Austin, here we come," Alex said. She gazed across the table at their mom. "We're all going to the game, right? You and Daddy promised."

"Of course!" Coach jumped in. "I need my family with me in Austin."

The championship game would be played two weeks from that night at the big university stadium in the state capital. Austin was a few hours away, so they'd have to stay overnight in a hotel. Ava hoped it would be a nice one with room service.

"Alex and I will check out all the cute boutiques and art galleries." Mrs. Sackett clapped her hands together.

"For sure!" Alex agreed, twirling a strand of her long, chocolate-brown hair.

Shopping was one of Alex's passions, but it certainly wasn't one of Ava's. Dressing rooms held the top spot on her "Most Hated Places" list. Give her a worn jersey over a dress and tights any day! The Sackett twins looked identical, except for Alex's long hair and Ava's short hair, but when it came to their likes and dislikes, they were polar opposites.

Belle Payton isn't a twin herself, but she does have twin brothers! She spent much of her childhood in the bleachers reading—er, cheering them on—at their football games. Though she left the South long ago to become a children's book editor in New York City, Belle still drinks approximately a gallon of sweet tea a week and loves treating her friends to her famous homemade mac-and-cheese. Belle is the author of many books for children and tweens and is currently having a blast writing two sides to each It Takes Two story.

More books about Alex and Ava?
That's **TWO** good to be true!

Available at your favorite store!